The Sleepover Club

Have you been invited to all these sleepovers?

1. The Sleepover Club at Frankie's
2. The Sleepover Club at Lyndsey's
3. The Sleepover Club at Felicity's
4. The Sleepover Club at Rosie's
5. The Sleepover Club at Kenny's
6. Starring the Sleepover Club
7. The Sleepover Girls go Spice
8. The 24 Hour Sleepover Club
9. The Sleepover Club Sleeps Out
10. Happy Birthday, Sleepover Club
11. Sleepover Girls on Horseback
12. Sleepover in Spain
13. Sleepover on Friday 13th
14. Sleepover Girls at Camp
15. Sleepover Girls go Detective
16. Sleepover Girls go Designer
17. The Sleepover Club Surfs the Net
18. Sleepover Girls on Screen
19. Sleepover Girls and Friends
20. Sleepover Girls on the Catwalk
21. The Sleepover Club Goes for Goal!
22. Sleepover Girls go Babysitting
23. Sleepover Girls go Snowboarding
24. Happy New Year, Sleepover Club!
25. Sleepover Club 2000
26. We Love You Sleepover Club
27. Vive le Sleepover Club!
28. Sleepover Club Eggstravaganza
29. Emergency Sleepover
30. Sleepover Girls on the Range
31. The Sleepover Club Bridesmaids
32. Sleepover Girls See Stars
33. Sleepover Club Blitz
34. Sleepover Girls in the Ring
35. Sari Sleepover

Merry Christmas Sleepover Club!

by Sue Mongredien

An imprint of HarperCollinsPublishers

The Sleepover Club ® is a
registered trademark of HarperCollins*Publishers* Ltd

First published in Great Britain by Collins in 2000
Collins is an imprint of HarperCollins*Publishers* Ltd
77-85 Fulham Palace Road, Hammersmith,
London, W6 8JB

The HarperCollins website address is
www.fireandwater.com

1 3 5 7 9 8 6 4 2

Text copyright © Sue Mongredien 2000

Original series characters, plotlines
and settings © Rose Impey 1997

ISBN 0 00675505 4

The author asserts the moral right to
be identified as the author of the work.

Printed and bound in Great Britain by
Omnia Books Limited,
Glasgow

Conditions of Sale
This book is sold subject to the condition
that it shall not, by way of trade or otherwise,
be lent, re-sold, hired out or otherwise circulated
without the publisher's prior consent in any form,
binding or cover other than that in which it is
published and without a similar condition
including this condition being imposed
on the subsequent purchaser.

Sleepover Kit List

1. Sleeping bag
2. Pillow
3. Pyjamas or a nightdress
4. Slippers
5. Toothbrush, toothpaste, soap etc
6. Towel
7. Teddy
8. A creepy story
9. Food for a midnight feast: chocolate, crisps, sweets, biscuits. In fact anything you like to eat.
10. Torch
11. Hairbrush
12. Hair things like a bobble or hairband, if you need them
13. Clean knickers and socks
14. Change of clothes for the next day
15. Sleepover diary and membership card

CHAPTER ONE

Merry Christmas! Hello, it's Rosie here of the Sleepover Club – and I'm just about to hang up my stocking as it's Christmas Eve. Excellent!!

I just *lurrrrrrve* Christmas, don't you? It's my absolute favourite time of the year. Summer is great because there's no school and you can stay out late at night, but December has got to be THE most exciting month of the year. You're just waiting and waiting for the 25th, and everyone's buying secret presents for each other, and we do lots of cool stuff at school to celebrate. Sometimes there's even snow, which is awesome!

The Sleepover Club

Now, you know me – the most down-to-earth person you'll ever meet. But even *I* think there's something just a teeny bit magical about Christmas. Do you know what I mean? It just feels like the one time in the year where ANYTHING could happen, when your wishes really might come true!

I was talking to the others about Christmas wishes the other day, and we were all saying what we'd want for Christmas, if we were each granted one wish. If you've never met the other four in the Sleepover Club, I thought it would be a cool way to introduce them, so here goes.

Frankie didn't have to think twice about her wish. "I wish I could go to Mars!" she shouted straight away. Frankie's nuts about space and sci-fi stuff, you see. We used to call her Spaceman for a while because she went completely nerdy about the whole thing – reading loads of books about outer space, building a model rocket launch in her bedroom, borrowing all the *Star Trek* films from the video shop... She even wrote to NASA in America asking if she could go on the next space mission! Yep, she's pretty hooked, all right!

Mind you, if any one of us five was ever going to be something amazing like a rocket scientist or astronaut, it would definitely be Frankie. She's really brainy, and she's also got this knack of coming up with totally cool ideas and plans for us to do. I can honestly say I've never met anyone like her in my life! As my mum says, "That girl's an original!"

Lyndz next. Well, the first wish she came up with was, "I'd love a horse!" as she's completely and utterly crazy about animals. She goes riding at a stables not far from Cuddington, where we all live, but has always wanted her own horse, ever since she was tiny. But then, as soon as she'd said that, she wanted to make another wish. "I wish all the animals in the world were happy, and none of them would suffer or be frightened ever again!"

If you hadn't guessed, Lyndz is a teeny bit soppy! But I'm glad about that, because if she wasn't, I might never have joined the Sleepover Club. You see, it was kind-hearted

Lyndz who took pity on me when I'd just joined Cuddington Primary School and didn't know a soul. She asked me to come along to a sleepover at Frankie's one night and that's how I met the others. So I've got a lot to thank her for!

Lyndz is one of the nicest, kindest people you'll ever meet, who'd do anything for anyone. Sometimes I wish I could be more like her, as I'm a bit sarcastic and impatient at times. You know when you just can't help saying something horrible and you want to bite your tongue off straight after you say it? I do that ALL the time – but Lyndz NEVER says anything mean. Still, I'm not saying she's a goody-goody or anything.

Fliss took a bit of time thinking about her wish. "We can wish for anything?" she said cautiously.

"Fliss, it's only a game," Frankie said impatiently. "Your fairy godmother isn't really going to come along and wave a wand, you know!"

"I know, I know!" Fliss said crossly. "I was only asking!"

Merry Christmas, Sleepover Club!

"So what's it going to be then, Flissy?" I asked. "Nose job? Modelling assignment?" (See? I told you I could be a bit sarky, didn't I?)

"A fairytale wedding with Ryan Scott, puke puke?" Kenny suggested, pulling a sick face.

Fliss tossed her long blonde hair back, looking a bit annoyed. "What do you mean, *nose job*?" she asked me. "What's wrong with my nose?"

"Er... nothing, nothing!" I said hastily. Fliss is a bit vain, you see, and doesn't take kindly to any criticism of the way she looks!

"I think I'd wish for £100 to spend on clothes," she said, her eyes lighting up at the thought. "No, wait – £1,000!" she said. Then she thought about it a bit more. "I wish I had a MILLION pounds to go on the most amazing shopping spree ever!"

She was positively beaming by now, whereas we were all staring at her, horrified at such a boring wish.

"Oh, I'd buy you all something too, of course!" she said, waving a hand casually.

"Wow, thanks, Fliss," Kenny said sarcastically. "Only if you're sure you can spare it, of course! You can't buy much with a million pounds these days, can you?"

Fliss looked annoyed. "Well, if you're going to be like that, I won't buy you *anything*!" she snapped. "I'll keep it all myself!"

Frankie rolled her eyes. "It's not a REAL wish, Fliss," she reminded her. "You don't really get to have your million pounds, you know!"

That's Fliss for you, anyway. Madly in love with clothes, make-up... and mirrors! She's the girliest one of us five and she sometimes gets on my nerves by being a bit wet and sappy, but she's also quite a laugh because you can wind her up a treat before she realises you're teasing her.

Kenny's turn next. "Well, my wish would be to wish for a billion other wishes!" she said craftily. "That way I can have whatever I want – whenever I want it!"

"You can't do that!" Fliss shouted at once. I think she was just gutted she hadn't thought of it first.

"It's my wish, I can ask for anything I like!" Kenny said, sticking her tongue out at her.

Merry Christmas, Sleepover Club!

"Just 'cos YOU wasted yours on boring shopping and boring clothes – DERRRR!"

Fliss scowled.

"No, seriously, though," Frankie said. "What would be the one thing you'd like most of all?"

Kenny's next answer was a tad predictable, really.

"I wish I could play for Leicester City and score the winning goal for them in the Cup Final," she sighed longingly. "That would just be *sooooo* cool!"

"Er, Kenz – you're a girl, mate," Frankie pointed out.

"I know, I know," Kenny said. "But that's part of the wish – that the team spot me playing footy in the park and realise I'm so mega-talented they'll have to bend the rules to let me play for them."

"Sounds a bit like Babe the pig where the farmer let Babe be in the sheepdog trials because he was so good," Lyndz said thoughtfully.

"Lyndz, if you're calling me a pig, I'll..." Kenny said warningly.

Lyndz giggled and put her hand up to her

mouth. "I wasn't!" she said. "Honest! But it wouldn't have been an insult anyway – pigs are lovely!"

In answer to that, Kenny started making piggy squeals and grunts and chased Lyndz around the room, until Lyndz collapsed in a giggling fit. Then "the pig" got down on all fours, still squealing, and starting nudging Lyndz with her head.

"S-s-s-stop it!" Lyndz panted, weakly trying to push her away. "P-p-pack it in, piggy!"

Anyway, yeah, so Kenny is mad on sport, especially football and swimming. She's captain of our netball team at school, but was really miffed when she couldn't play cricket with the boys. She even went to the head teacher about it, saying it was unfair and sexist! I think she really wishes she was actually a boy sometimes.

Kenny has energy and enthusiasm like you've never seen before. Sometimes we call her "the power station" because she's like a one-woman generator! Her and Frankie are a good match in that way. They both hate sitting still and prefer to be bouncing around somewhere outside. No wonder they're both so skinny.

The other thing you should know about Kenny is that she's a complete gore-hound. She just loves blood and guts and gross stuff like that. She wants to be a doctor when she's older, like her dad. Already, she knows lots of amazing things about the way things work in your body, and loves telling us all the yuckiest stuff to try and gross us out. Fliss usually kicks up a fuss before too long as she's mega-squeamish, and even the word "blood" makes her feel sick (so she says). I think that just encourages Kenny to find even more horrible things to tell us about, though.

I was the last one to make my wish. I just couldn't decide. Part of me wished we had a nicer house to live in. Ours is a complete dump, ever since my dad moved out before he'd had a chance to do it up. I used to get a bit embarrassed about letting the others come round because it was so scruffy, and there's still loads that needs doing to it even now – I mean, we still haven't got carpets in some rooms. Me and the gang ended up decorating my room last year because I got so sick of just having bare plaster walls in there. Dad was originally going to paint my room for me, but... I guess he had other things on his mind.

"Come on, Rosie!" Lyndz was saying, elbowing me. "You've had ages to think about it now!"

"Yeah, what's your gut instinct?" Kenny asked. "What was the first thing that popped into your head?"

"I wish Adam could walk," I said straight out. Adam's my brother and he's in a wheelchair. He's a really lovely brother (apart from when he takes the mickey out of me, of course) and he's never been able to walk or talk properly. Sometimes I catch sight of his face if I'm going off on my bike, and he just has this sad look in his eyes which makes me feel really *guilty* that my legs work OK and I don't even think about them. Or sometimes he'll be watching sport on telly, and I just know that he's thinking about how he'll never be able to play football or rugby or... You know. I mean, I've grown up with him, so I'm used to it, and obviously he is, too – but it's still sad.

Merry Christmas, Sleepover Club!

The others were a bit quiet when I said my wish. Kenny's great with Adam, she just treats him like a normal boy and has a laugh with him about stuff, but I know the others feel a bit awkward around him. Fliss, especially – I think she's a bit scared of Adam, to be honest. I suppose if you're not used to being around someone who's disabled, you don't quite know how to react at first.

"That's a nice wish," Lyndz said in the end. "That would be lovely if it came true."

"Yeah," I said. I felt a bit bad that everyone had gone so quiet and thoughtful because of me. "But I also wish my mum would find a new bloke now! A nice new boyfriend for the new year, that would be wicked. Especially if he was rich!"

"Ooh, that would be good," said Fliss thoughtfully. She likes anything to do with what she calls "affairs of the heart". "Your mum's quite pretty – I'm sure she'd be able to find someone nice."

"Do we know anyone we could fix her up with?" Frankie joked, raising an eyebrow at me.

"Not Dishy Dave again, after the Brown Owl disaster!" Lyndz said with a shudder. "That was awful!"

We all giggled, remembering our terrible attempt to fix up Brown Owl with Dave, the school caretaker. It had gone about as wrong as it could have!

"I'm definitely not putting my mum through that!" I said firmly. "In fact, I totally intend to stay OUT of her love life, so don't you lot get any ideas!"

Frankie's face fell, and I could tell she'd been half-serious about plotting to fix my mum up. "Well, if you're sure..." she said reluctantly. "We do have quite a hunky next-door neighbour who's just moved in – no girlfriend, either!"

"No, thanks!" I said, shaking my head. "End of discussion, Frankie!"

Anyway, you've hopefully got a good idea of what we're all like now. We're all best friends and do lots of stuff together. We have a sleepover once a week, on a Friday or Saturday, and take it in turns to host it. Wherever we have the sleepover, it's always

Merry Christmas, Sleepover Club!

an excellent laugh. There's not much sleep involved though, what with all the games we play and sweets we munch!

What I like most of all, though, is having four really close friends who I can have a laugh with, be myself with and trust with all my secrets. I've never had that before, and it's absolutely ACE! Sure, we sometimes bicker and fall out about stupid things, but at the end of the day, I don't know how I'd get along without them. Well, that's the Sleepover Club for you!

CHAPTER TWO

I'd better get on with the story, now you've met everyone.

I suppose it all started in the last week of November, when Mrs Weaver came into the classroom and announced that our class and Mr Nicholls' class would be putting on a Christmas pantomime of Cinderella for the parents and the rest of the school.

There was this big excited OOOOH! from all of us. Excellent! Normally we only ever do a boring nativity play and a carol concert. I don't know about you, but singing *Little Donkey* is NOT my idea of a good time. But Mrs Weaver went on to say that Miss

Merry Christmas, Sleepover Club!

Middleton, the new infant teacher who'd come to our school in September, was a bit of a creative sort. Not only had she written the pantomime, but she'd also agreed to organise the whole thing. COO-ELL!

Us five grinned and made thumbs-up signs at each other. Miss Middleton was really young and pretty and funny. This could turn out to be an ace Sleepover Club event!

The classroom was buzzing as everyone started whispering things to each other in excitement. Mrs Weaver banged on her desk with a ruler. "Quieten down!" she called. "Do you want me to tell you how to audition for the panto, or not?!"

Instantly, everyone was as quiet as mice.

Mrs Weaver smiled. "Oh, that got your attention, didn't it?" she said. "Seeing as I obviously have a class of budding actors and actresses, I'd better tell you that there's a meeting in the hall at lunchtime today, for everyone interested in taking part. And for those of you who AREN'T interested in being on the stage, let me remind you that we'll need lots of scenery painters, costume designers, prop makers and people to help out with the lighting, too! So if you want to sign up for anything, come along to the hall at one o'clock sharp."

We all grinned at each other. This was going to be wicked!

Fliss put her hand up, blushing slightly. "Er, Mrs Weaver, who gets to be Cinderella?" she asked, tossing her long hair.

Kenny rolled her eyes. "Let me guess – you think it should be YOU!" she muttered.

Mrs Weaver frowned at Kenny, and then turned her attention to Fliss. "Well, Felicity, that's why we're having auditions," she said. "Miss Middleton will tell us more about it at lunchtime, but basically, anyone who's interested in being Cinderella will have to do an audition next week. For the audition, you'll have to read out some of Cinderella's lines and maybe sing a song, too, so we can see who has a good voice, and who can speak nice and clearly."

Fliss bit her lip. "But Cinderella IS blonde, isn't she?" she said, frowning. "I thought—"

"The Cinderella in the Disney cartoon is

blonde, yes," Mrs Weaver said firmly. "But we're not going to choose our Cinderella on hair colour, Felicity – just talent!"

"Oh, of course," Fliss said, sounding a bit dejected. I knew – and the whole class knew – that Fliss had thought she'd get the part on looks alone!

"She's got no chance, then, if they're going for talent!" whispered Emily Berryman loudly. Snidey cow!!

If you didn't know, her and her snotty sidekick Emma Hughes are big enemies of the Sleepover Club. We call them the M&Ms, but that's certainly not because they're as nice as the chocolate M&Ms. They're the sort of girls who'll pull your ponytail really hard, or nick your nicest pen when they think you're not looking. I'm sure there's a couple like them in your class, too, worse luck!

That morning seemed to go really *really* slo-o-ow. I swear time stood still and we were trapped in the classroom for about a week. Mrs Weaver was teaching us this complicated thing about fractions which I just couldn't understand. Every time I looked down at my maths book, the same thought popped into my head. *Cinderella! Cinderella! Cinderella!*

I was dying for lunchtime to come, so we could go to Miss Middleton's meeting and hear all about the panto. How could anyone concentrate on boring fractions at a time like this?

I *love* the story of Cinderella. OK, so the ending's a bit sloppy with Prince Charming and all that yucky lovey-dovey stuff, but I just adore the bit where the fairy godmother turns the pumpkin into a magnificent carriage, and the four mice into beautiful white horses. Wouldn't that be awesome, having a real-life fairy godmother who came into your bedroom and magicked everything up for you? But how on earth was Miss Middleton going to make that happen on stage? Unless she—

"Rosie Cartwright! Are you with us?" came Mrs Weaver's voice. "Have you lost the power of your ears, suddenly?"

I went bright red. Oops! Caught daydreaming! "Sorry," I said, staring down at my page again.

"We were talking about expressing the

fraction two-thirds as a decimal," Mrs Weaver said, still not finished with me. "Would you care to share your thoughts on that with us?"

"Er..." I said, hoping a flash of inspiration would strike. But wouldn't you know, it didn't. I'm TERRIBLE at maths! "Er... I don't know, Miss," I said in the end, feeling a bit of an idiot.

"You don't know, Miss," repeated Mrs Weaver. "I see. You don't know the answer, even though I've just spent ten minutes explaining it to the rest of the class who WERE listening. Now if I was feeling really mean, I'd tell you to stay in at lunchtime for some extra work on fractions..."

I stared at her in horror. She couldn't be so evil, surely?

"... but luckily for you, I'll let you off – provided you pay attention for the rest of the lesson. Do we have ourselves a deal?"

"Deal," I gulped gratefully, vowing to be a model pupil for the rest of the morning. There was no way I wanted to miss that lunchtime meeting!

"Good," said Mrs Weaver. "So who CAN tell me the answer, then?"

Smug keen-bean Emma Hughes stuck her hand straight up. Surprise, surprise! Couldn't resist a chance to make one of the Sleepover Club look bad in front of the teacher, as usual.

Wouldn't you know it, the morning went even *slower* now I actually had to pay attention and do some work. About three years later, it was lunchtime. We wolfed down our sandwiches in the dining hall, then charged along to the pantomime meeting in the main hall – along with practically everyone else in our year! The joint was JUMPING, as Frankie would say.

Miss Middleton stood at the front with a clipboard. Mrs Weaver, Mr Nicholls and Mrs Somersby were also standing around, holding pieces of paper with lists printed on them.

"Hello, everyone," Miss Middleton said, when we'd all quietened down. "What a great turn-out! I'm delighted so many of you are interested in helping out on this year's pantomime. As your teachers have no doubt told you, we're going to be putting on two performances of Cinderella. There's plenty of work for everyone to get involved with, so

Merry Christmas, Sleepover Club!

we'll need lots of helping hands."

She cleared her throat, and then looked serious.

"Now, this is going to be the first meeting of many, between now and Christmas. There are going to be LOTS of rehearsals, too, so if you're already busy with things like football or swimming clubs, please make sure you're not taking on too much. We don't want anyone collapsing with exhaustion right before Christmas, do we?"

I saw Kenny look a bit thoughtful at that. She's in the Cuddington Swimming Club and trains twice a week and sometimes on Saturday mornings, too. Still, as Kenny didn't seem to know the meaning of the word "exhaustion", I guessed she would probably manage to combine that with the panto quite easily!

"Now, like I said, taking on a part in the play will mean a lot of work, but it's also going to be a lot of fun," Miss Middleton said, smiling around at everyone. "Does everyone know the story of Cinderella? Good. Well, what we'll do next is try and organise everyone into groups.

Mr Nicholls has kindly agreed to be in charge of props, scenery and lighting, and Mrs Somersby is going to be sorting out all the costumes and make-up. Last but not least, Mrs Weaver and I will be running the auditions and coaching the rehearsals. Got that?"

"Yes!" everyone chorused.

"Excellent!" said Miss Middleton. "If you're interested in helping with props and scenery, go and stand in that corner with Mr Nicholls. If you want to help with costumes and make-up, go and stand in THAT corner with Mrs Somersby. And if you'd like an acting, singing or dancing part, stay where you are."

There was bedlam as lots of people got up and started making their way to different parts of the hall.

The five of us looked at each other.

"I quite fancy a go at making props..." said Kenny.

"I wouldn't mind doing make-up," Frankie said thoughtfully. "I can do some wicked designs, I've been practising!"

"Oh, let's stick together!" Lyndz said. "It'll be much more fun if we're *all* acting in it!"

"Yeah, Lyndz is right," I said. "Why don't we all go in for the auditions? It would be a right laugh!"

"What do you think, Fliss?" Kenny asked. "Don't you fancy having a go on the lighting or carpentry?"

Fliss shuddered, and the rest of us laughed. Not likely! Fliss thinks anything technical is "man's work" – and anyway, she might break a nail doing something like that.

"No, thanks!" she said, feelingly. Then she smiled serenely. "Anyway, I'm going to be Cinderella. I just know I'm going to get the part!"

"Ooh, very modest of you to say so, Fliss," Frankie joked. "Should I ask for your autograph now, or when you're REALLY famous?!"

"Fliss, EVERYONE's going to be going for Cinderella," Lyndz said tactfully. "You don't know for sure you'll get the part, do you?"

Fliss tossed her hair back, looking a bit peeved. "Don't tell me *you're* going for the part as well, then?" she asked.

Lyndz shook her head. "Nah," she admitted. "Actually, there's another part I'd rather play..."

"What?" I asked in interest. I hadn't had Lyndz down as the dramatic type before.

She went a bit pink. "Well... you know that bit where the fairy godmother magicks everything so Cinderella can go to the ball?" she said.

"Ye-e-e-e-es," we said.

"Ahh, you want to be the fairy godmother?" Kenny asked.

"No," Lyndz said.

"The pumpkin?" Fliss said – rather cattily, actually, as Lyndz is a teeny bit plump.

"No, one of the horses!" Lyndz said, looking a bit embarrassed. "Oh, don't laugh, it's what I want to be!"

Too late – we all started roaring with laughter! Of all the things to wish to be in the pantomime!

"Don't worry, I'm sure there won't be much competition to be a horse," I spluttered.

"No, it's not like it's the MANE part or anything!" Kenny giggled.

Luckily for Lyndz, Miss Middleton clapped her hands for quiet just then and we all had to bite our lips to stop ourselves laughing any more.

There were still a lot of people left in the hall, even when Mr Nicholls and Mrs Somersby had taken their volunteers off to different rooms. It looked like *everyone* wanted to be treading the boards this Christmas.

"First of all, I'm going to tell you the cast list of the pantomime, so you can start thinking about what you'd like to go for," Miss Middleton said, when everyone was listening. "Here goes – Cinderella, her stepmother Wicked Wilma, the two Ugly Sisters Grizzle and Moana, Buttons, Prince Charming, Angelica the fairy godmother, and a narrator. They're the main characters, and auditions will be held for those parts on Monday lunchtime in my classroom."

Emma Hughes smirked at Fliss. "Ever thought about trying out for one of the Ugly Sisters?" she said. "I reckon you'd get it easily!"

Fliss looked as if she was about to burst into tears, but Kenny, as ever, was straight in there.

"Shame there aren't any DOGS in Cinderella," she said, eyes glittering. "You and your poochy mate might actually get picked to do something then!"

"Girls, please!" called Miss Middleton. "We've a lot to get through today. Right, so those are the main parts. We'll also need dancers for the ball scene, a chorus, Prince Charming's butler, and some people to be Cinderella's horses and coachman. And there'll be an open audition for those parts on Tuesday lunchtime, in my classroom."

Fliss stuck her hand in the air. "Please, Miss, what will we have to do at the auditions?" she asked.

"Good question," said Miss Middleton. "I'll give you a page from the script and we'll practise acting it out in pairs. Anyone who wants to be Cinderella or the fairy godmother must have a good singing voice as there will be a couple of songs for you in the show. I think that's it for now. See you all next week, I hope!"

The hall broke out into an excited chatter. It all sounded like it was going to be excellent fun!

"I can't wait for next Monday!" said Fliss, with her serene smile again. Honestly, I'd never known Fliss to be so confident about anything before!

"First things first," I said. "We've got to have a Cinderella sleepover to practise for the audition, and talk about what parts we all want to do."

"Deffo!" Kenny said. "How about at mine? We haven't been there for ages."

"Agreed!" said Frankie. "I'll bring my greasepaint along so we can look the part!"

"And I'll bring some of the dressing-up clothes!" Lyndz promised.

"Cool!" Kenny said. "It's a date!"

CHAPTER THREE

There's nothing like a good sleepover to start the weekend with a bang! Everyone was really looking forward to this one, too. I mean, sleepovers are always excellent, but when we've got something really special coming up, like the pantomime, it makes it even more fun.

By the end of Friday afternoon, none of us could think about doing any work – we were all too excited about the evening ahead. Luckily, on Friday afternoons, Mrs Weaver always reads to us, so you don't have to concentrate too hard. This time she took out a copy of *Matilda* by Roald

Merry Christmas, Sleepover Club!

Dahl, so we all got to sit and listen to that. It was such a good story, I actually managed to STOP thinking about Cinderella and sleepovers for a while – but only just!

Then all of a sudden it was three-thirty and time to go. Yippeeee! Me and Fliss were going straight back to Kenny's house with her, while Lyndz and Frankie were going to go home and pick up their bags of goodies first, then come over a bit later. Kenny doesn't live far from the school, so we all walked back – stopping at the sweet shop first, of course.

We don't seem to have that many sleepovers at Kenny's, partly because of her horrid older sister, Molly Moany-guts, who Kenny shares a room with. Whenever we have a sleepover, Molly has to move in with Emma, their oldest sister, for the night. And boy, does Molly kick up a stink about it! She makes a real fuss if we so much as TOUCH any of her stuff, so I'm always a bit worried about breaking something of hers, especially when Kenny sets up one of her famous assault courses round the bedroom.

This time, we'd just left the sweet shop

when we heard a familiar horrible voice.

"Ahh, look! It's the Bedtime Club for little girly-wirlies!"

You guessed it – Molly and her equally horrible friend, Carli, sniggering so hard they looked as if they were about to wet their pants.

Fliss looked a bit rattled. She hates scenes, especially in public, where someone might see her. "Ignore them, Kenny," she hissed. "Come on, let's go."

Ignore them? Fat chance! Kenny doesn't know the meaning of the word "ignore" when it comes to miserable Molly. She turned round at once, eyes sparkling, ready for battle.

"Ahh, look! Battersea Dogs' Home have let some strays loose because they were so hideous, nobody wanted them!" she said sweetly. "Here, doggies! Come here!"

Molly took a step forward. BIG mistake!

"Oh, look, they're so obedient, they even come when I call them!" Kenny cooed in delight. "Good doggy!"

Molly glared at her younger sister and folded her arms across her chest. "You think you're so clever, don't you, LAURA?" she said, using Kenny's real (hated) name, the name that only teachers and parents are allowed to use.

"I think, therefore I am," Kenny shot back. "Shame YOU haven't learned how to think yet, big mouth!"

"You've had it!" Molly snapped. "C'mon, Carli – let's get 'em!"

"Run!!" yelled Kenny as they both came charging towards us.

Fliss and I didn't need telling twice, and we sprinted off at once. Luckily, all three of us are pretty fast, and after a couple of minutes, Molly and Carli gave up the chase and just shouted a few horrible things after us up the street.

"What did you have to do that for, Kenny?" grumbled Fliss, patting her hair anxiously. Fliss is actually quite good at running because she's got long legs, but she hates getting hot and bothered because it messes her hair up.

"For fun, of course!" grinned Kenny. "Didn't I ever tell you our family motto? It's *Meanus Sisteris*."

"What does that mean?" Fliss asked, looking puzzled.

"Be mean to your sisters," Kenny said solemnly. "So I try my hardest, whenever I can."

"Really?" Fliss asked. "That's a bit weird!"

Kenny and I rolled our eyes at each other, trying not to giggle. Fliss was just TOO easy to wind up sometimes!

"Of course, there's also the other family motto – *Fibius Flisseratum*," Kenny said, biting her lip. "Did I ever tell you that one?"

"No," said Fliss, all wide-eyed. "What does that mean?"

I could hardly watch! Fliss was just SO gullible, it was untrue!

"It means, tell lies to people called Fliss," Kenny said, trying to keep a straight face.

It was no good – I started giggling helplessly. Kenny is such an excellent wind-up merchant!

Fliss looked puzzled. "You mean..." she started – and then she finally clocked what was going on. "Kenny!" she said, swinging her bag at her indignantly. "Did you just make that up? Did you?"

There was no reply. Me and Kenny were both snorting with laughter, leaning against someone's garden wall.

"You did, didn't you?" Fliss said crossly. "Well! Of all the—"

"It was only a joke," Kenny spluttered weakly. "I couldn't resist... *Fibius Flisseratum* – I'll have to remember that!"

We were nearly at Kenny's house now, and we'd spent so long messing around and giggling that Molly and Carli had caught up with us.

"Oh, look who it isn't," Kenny muttered under her breath.

"Is Carli sleeping over tonight as well?" I asked. It was going to be a pretty full house, if so!

Kenny pulled one of her sickest faces. "Afraid so," she said. "You know Molly. Can't bear to be left out of anything, even having friends round. Luckily Emma's staying over with one of HER friends, so Molly and Carli are both in Emma's bedroom tonight." She lowered her voice. "I THINK Molly's just got a boyfriend, believe it or not, so hopefully they'll be chatting about that all night and they won't be bugging us!"

"That would be a first," Fliss said gloomily.

"Well, it IS, as far as I know," Kenny said, deadpan. "No-one's ever asked her out before!"

"What about Edward Marsh?" I asked. "I thought she was dead keen on him for a while."

"Nah, they were just mates," Kenny smirked. "Like he would really fancy that monster, anyway!"

Edward Marsh was this horrible, annoying boy who'd ganged up with Molly against us on our circus skills course at half-term. (Now there's a Sleepover story to look out for!)

Kenny leaped on to Fliss's back as we were coming up the path. "Giddy-up, horsey!" she told her.

Just then, Kenny's mum opened the front door. "Hello, girls!" she smiled. Kenny's mum is VERY smiley and gentle – totally unlike her youngest daughter! "Laura, what on earth are you doing to Felicity? The neighbours must think the circus is back in town!"

"Yeah, with Molly as the talking chimp this time," Kenny said quietly – but loud enough for her mum to hear.

"That'll do!" Mrs McKenzie said, half-sternly, half-smiling. "Now come in, it's freezing! I'll make you some hot chocolate."

We'd just polished off a load of hot chocolate and Jaffa Cakes when Frankie and Lyndz turned up with big carrier bags of stuff. So then we had to have a load more hot chocolate and Jaffa Cakes, just to keep them company, of course. Once we were all feeling completely stuffed, we went up to Kenny's room to get away from Molly Monster-Features and creepy Carli. As usual, there was a handwritten note on Molly's side of the room:

LAURA: Don't touch my stuff – don't even look at it! Molly

"Yeah, yeah, like we're scared!" Kenny said casually, ripping the note up and tossing it into the bin.

"Let's get down to business!" Frankie said.

"I've brought along lots of groovy make-up so we can do ourselves up as our characters."

"And I've got a load of clothes here as well," Lyndz said, dumping two huge bags on Kenny's bed. "But I couldn't find a horse costume for me – just these brown jodhpurs and a brown jumper."

"I can make your face up to look like a horse!" Frankie said at once.

"Right, well, I'll be Cinderella, then," Fliss said decisively.

"Hang on a minute," I said, feeling my cheeks going a bit red. "I wouldn't mind being Cinderella either, so—"

"YOU?" Fliss said, sounding astonished. "But you haven't even got long hair!"

Well, she'd got me on that one. I've got quite short, brown hair in a bob and a stubby nose and freckles, so I suppose I didn't exactly look the part. But I'd been thinking about it all week and I'd decided I was going to go for Cinderella as well. Why not? Reach for the moon, as my mum always tells me.

Kenny groaned. "Fliss, being Cinderella isn't just about having long hair, you know," she said. "Remember what Mrs Weaver said? They'll be going on talent, not looks. And anyway, Rosie could always wear a wig if she got the part!"

"Oh, so you think Rosie's going to get the part, do you?" Fliss said. She sounded all sniffy, as if she was going to cry. "Charming!"

"Kenny, what part are you going to go for?" Frankie said, changing the subject. I shot her a grateful look. There was no way Fliss was going to stop me going for Cinderella just because SHE wanted to be it. And if she thought she could give me a guilt trip about it, she had another think coming!

"One of the Ugly Sisters, maybe," Kenny said, and we all laughed. "No, seriously!" she said. "It's probably going to be quite a funny part, right? And I don't want anything serious or soppy to do. I'd prefer to make everyone laugh."

As she was saying this, I could just imagine Kenny in a horrible outfit and wig, clowning around on stage and making the audience laugh, just like she had done on our circus course. She'd be perfect in the part!

"How about you, Frank?" I asked. "No aliens in Cinderella for you to play!"

"Shame," she said, sounding serious. "I wouldn't mind being an Ugly Sister, too – but what I'd REALLY like to be is Wicked Wilma, the evil old stepmother. Then I'd get to boss the Ugly Sisters around and make Cinderella cry!"

I laughed at that but Fliss looked a bit fearful.

"That's not very nice!" she pouted.

"THAT's the point, derr-brain!" Frankie said. "I'm meant to be horrible, aren't I?"

"This is going to be such a laugh," Lyndz said happily. "I'm so glad they picked a pantomime that has horses in it! I've already asked Miss Middleton if I could be one of the horses, and she said that would be fine. Isn't that cool?!"

"Awesome," I said, trying not to smile. "So shall we practise for our auditions or what?"

"Oh, good idea!" said Fliss, jumping up. "I've prepared something already, actually." She raised her eyebrows at me, as if to say, *Bet you haven't!*

Merry Christmas, Sleepover Club!

She pulled a piece of paper out of her bag, and was about to start when she fixed me with a hard stare. "Maybe Rosie shouldn't be in the room while I do this," she said. "I don't want her copying the way I do my audition piece."

Kenny threw a Curly Wurly at her. "Get a grip, Fliss!" she said. "Stop being a prima donna and get on with it!"

"I'm nothing like Madonna!" Fliss snapped back at her, tossing her hair over her shoulders.

"No, she meant... Oh, never mind," said Frankie wearily. "Just dazzle us with your talent!"

Fliss cleared her throat. "Now, obviously, I don't have a proper page from the pantomime script, like we will in the audition," she said primly. "So I've just written a few lines that Cinderella might say, OK? It's the bit where Cinders is at home while the Ugly Sisters have gone off to the ball, just before the fairy—"

"Yeah, yeah!" Kenny said impatiently. "Let's hear it, then!"

Fliss knelt down on the floor, tossed her hair back again and put one hand in front of her, almost as if she was begging.

"Oh, woe!" she began. "Woe is me! Here all alone on the night of the ball, when handsome Prince Charming will choose a bride!"

She paused dramatically and Lyndz started clapping. Fliss glared at her. "I haven't finished yet!" she snapped.

"Oops! Sorry!" said Lyndz. "It's very good, though!"

Fliss had a quick look at her piece of paper then continued, flourishing her hand theatrically. "Oh, woe! It's all dark, and there are horrible rats scratching around me! And I must do all this cleaning while those mean sisters of mine are dancing around in their best dresses! Oh, woe! If only I had a fairy godmother!"

She collapsed on the floor, one hand still outstretched, and was motionless. The four of us looked at each other, trying not to giggle. Was that the end yet? Dared we clap this time?

After about twenty seconds, Fliss sat up gracefully and bowed.

"That was really good, Fliss," Lyndz said warmly.

"Yes, Rosie must be dead worried after seeing that audition piece," Kenny said sarcastically.

"Oh, I am," I assured her, crossing my fingers behind my back.

Fliss looked pleased with herself. "Thank you," she said modestly. "I did practise it a LOT last night, to be honest, that's probably why it's so good."

"Mmm, probably," Frankie said, looking at the floor. "What about a song, though? What are you going to sing?"

"I thought I'd sing that song from *Titanic*, you know, by Celine Dion," Fliss said.

"What, *My Fart Will Go On*?" Kenny asked. "Always reminds me of my dad, that one..."

"Kenny!" Fliss giggled. "It's *My* HEART *Will Go On*! Anyway, what do you think?"

And with that, she launched into the chorus at top volume. Omigosh – ever heard a cat yowl when you tread on its tail by mistake? Fliss sounded even more pained than that! It was terrible!! To shut her up, Kenny waited until Fliss was singing a really long high note, with her mouth wide open, and then threw a marshmallow straight in there. Glug! That brought her to a stop!

"Well, like you said, you really are NOTHING like Madonna," Frankie mused. She meant it teasingly of course, but said it in a nice voice, so Fliss just looked confused.

"Thanks," she said uncertainly. Then she looked around at the rest of us. "Well?" she demanded. "What do you think? Am I going to be Cinderella, or what?"

"Mmmm... Maybe... Fingers crossed," everyone said politely, including me. But inside I was feeling a bit smug. There was NO WAY Fliss was going to be Cinderella – not with a voice like that!

CHAPTER FOUR

After Fliss's eye-opening performance, the rest of us took turns to dress up and try out different stuff for our audition pieces. No-one else had rehearsed or written anything like Fliss had – we all did it off the cuff. I hadn't done much drama before at school, but found I was really enjoying myself, both watching the others and taking part.

Kenny did a wickedly funny skit as an Ugly Sister who was getting ready for the ball. She had us all rolling about laughing as she primped up the big purple wig Lyndz had brought along, put face powder on her warts and pouted at herself in the mirror. The more we laughed, the funnier Kenny became. It was as if she instinctively knew how to play to the audience.

"I feel pretty, oh so pretty!" she sang into the mirror, in this horrible croak. She was excellent!

Then Frankie took a turn as the wicked stepmother, having a go at Cinders for not cleaning the kitchen floor properly. She made her face up to look like an old granny, put curlers and a headscarf on her head, and pulled herself up to her full height, so as to look as scary and mean as possible.

Then she pursed up her mouth and let rip, and I nearly jumped out of my skin! Frankie's never normally in a bad mood, so it was quite scary, seeing her being so aggressive and nasty.

"Cinders, you lazy good-for-nothing hussy!" she yelled, glaring ferociously at us. "If I wanted something useless in my kitchen, I'd get an ornament! But you – YOU – are meant to clean this place! Do you know what clean means? I said, *do you know what clean means?*"

Frankie was yelling right into Fliss's face, who flinched. "Er... n-n-n-o," she stammered.

"Ha!" sneered Frankie. "You DO surprise me! Here, watch this!"

At that point, Frankie started flinging her arms around in the air.

"What's that?" Kenny asked.

"I'm throwing bags of rice all over the floor, just to be mean," Frankie said in her normal voice. Then Wicked Wilma's voice came back. "See that? That's a mess, that is. And when I come back, I want it all cleaned up, you hear? Clean, clean, CLEAN!"

Frankie threw herself on the bed as we all clapped.

"You are one wicked stepmother," I told her, admiringly.

"You are a cow!" Kenny agreed, sounding respectful. "No wonder Cinders cuts all her hair off in despair!"

Fliss looked anxious at that. "Does she? I don't remember that bit."

"Yeah!" Kenny said, straight-faced. "She gives herself a skinhead, trying to disguise herself as the bald chef, don't you remember?"

"No!" Fliss said, shaking her head. She was looking REALLY anxious now, at the thought of being a skinhead Cinderella!

"Fliss, she's only messing about," Lyndz said.

"AGAIN!" Kenny grinned. "Fliss, you're making it too easy for me tonight."

Fliss pulled a face and nibbled on a Loveheart. "We haven't seen Rosie's piece yet," she said, giving me a challenging look. Blimey, she was feeling competitive! Obviously it had really narked her that I'd decided to go for the part of Cinderella as well as her.

"OK, here's my song," I said. I'd decided to sing one of my mum's favourite old songs, *That Old Devil Called Love*. Not because it has anything to do with Cinderella, but just because it's kind of sad and slow, and I'd thought it might suit the mood.

"It's that old devil called love again..." I sang. I haven't got a fantastic singing voice or anything, but I can hold a note at least and our music teacher at school says I have good pitch, whatever that means. I felt a bit embarrassed at first, singing in front of the others, but it's such a great song, I closed my eyes and just got into it. When I finished, the others all clapped and cheered me.

"Girl, you can SING!" Frankie said in an American accent. "That was brilliant, Rosie!"

"Not bad," Fliss sniffed critically. Oh well – I was never expecting any praise from HER!

Then I did my audition piece. I was dreading it a bit, after seeing such a flop from Fliss, then two such hilarious ones from Frankie and Kenny. I decided to just play it straight, and do a scene where Cinderella is confiding in Buttons.

"Those sisters, they're not just ugly, they're so horrible as well!" I started. "The other day I caught Grizzle putting itching powder in my knicker drawer, and when I confronted her, do you know what she said?"

"No!" called out Lyndz, getting into it.

"She told me it was talcum powder to make my clothes smell nice! Well, of course, I didn't believe a word of it! So do you know what I did, then?"

"NO!" the others all called out.

"Well, I waited until she'd gone out

shopping with Moana, then I swapped all our knickers around so that if it WAS itching powder, THEY'D get it! You should have seen them the next day, Buttons – ants in the pants, or what? They were rolling around, scratching away like you've never seen before!"

I'd only just got going when Fliss interrupted me.

"Rosie, don't you think it's a bit VULGAR to talk about knickers in your audition piece?" she said disapprovingly.

"I'll be reading from the script in the audition, won't I, you derr-bo?" I said scathingly. "I won't REALLY be saying all this!"

"Knickers are more interesting than 'woe is me' anyway," said Kenny. "At least Rosie's Cinderella had a bit of life in her, she wasn't just flopping about on the stage like a dying fish!"

Fliss went bright red and shut her mouth tightly. "That's what YOU think, Kenny," she started. "Let me tell you—"

"Aaaaaand... moving on, let's change the subject," Lyndz said swiftly. "Shall we have a game of something?"

Merry Christmas, Sleepover Club!

"Yeah, good idea," Frankie said. "That was great, by the way, Rosie."

"Thanks," I said, feeling a bit cross with Fliss for interrupting me like that. Talk about spoiled brat. She just couldn't handle it if she wasn't getting her own way!

"Well, I think we're all set for the auditions," Kenny said, catching my eye. I could tell she knew how I was feeling. "And I say, just like in football, all's fair in love and war!"

"What?" said Fliss, frowning at her.

"I mean, Fliss," Kenny said, speaking extra-slowly, "may the best man – or girl – win! And let's not have any sulking or bad feelings because that's just boring."

"How about Hide and Seek?" Lyndz said diplomatically, as Fliss's chin wobbled a bit.

No bad feelings, indeed! I thought to myself. If Fliss didn't get her precious part, there would be a LOT of bad feeling, directed at whoever got to be Cinderella!

"How about Spy On Molly And Find Out Who The Unlucky Boyfriend Is?" Kenny suggested, eyes gleaming at the thought. "Go on, let's! I'm dying to find out. Just think how much teasing material I'll have once I know which loser she's got her sticky mitts on!"

Once Kenny's got her mind set on something, it's difficult to talk her out of it. Anyway, it sounded like fun to me. One of my favourite hobbies at home is earwigging on my big sister Tiffany's phone calls, especially when boys are involved. Some of those conversations are just hilarious!

Under Kenny's strict instructions, we all tiptoed along the corridor and stood in a huddle outside Molly's room. Kenny had brought along her Walkman, and, holding it up to the door, she pressed the Record button and gave us all a big happy wink. There was nothing Kenny liked more than getting one over on Molly.

Sure enough, Molly and Carli were deep in conversation.

"... And then he kissed me, right, and..."

"Ooh! What was it like?"

"Well, it was kind of soft and nice but... well, I didn't really know what to do, so I just sort of put my arms around him, on his back..."

"Really?"

"Yeah – ooh, he has a lovely back! Dead muscly!"

"And how long did you kiss for?"

"Only a few minutes – then you'll never guess what, Mr Graham came round the back of the science lab and caught us!"

"No!"

"I swear!"

"Nightmare!"

"Tell me about it!"

Kenny pulled a face at us, shaking her head. "Bor-ring!" she mouthed.

"So then Andrew said he had to go..."

We all looked at each other and grinned. Andrew, eh?!

"So has he asked you out, properly, like?"

"Yeah! That's the best bit! We're going to the pictures tomorrow afternoon!"

Kenny raised her eyebrows at that, and looked pleased with herself. That was good information to have up her sleeve!

"Ooh, are you going to sit in the back row?"

"Too right we are!"

Unable to resist keeping quiet any longer, Kenny suddenly sang out, "Molly and Andrew sitting in a tree, K-I-S-S-I-N-G!" Then she put on this silly high voice. "Ooh, he has EVER such a muscly back, you know!"

And then we all pegged it back to Kenny's room, quick as anything, giggling our heads off.

"You nosey BRATS!" Molly yelled, storming in the room after us. "You'd better not tell Mum about that!"

"What's it worth?" Kenny asked, smiling sweetly.

"Well, I WON'T kick your head in, if you don't say anything, put it like that!" Molly growled.

"Ooh, I hope you don't speak to Andy-Pandy loverboy like that," Kenny said, solemnly. "Not very feminine, is it, Mols?"

"Just zip it, all right?" Molly snapped, poking Kenny in the ribs. "And don't spy on us again, you losers! Don't you have better things to do?"

With that, she flung herself out of the room, slamming the door behind her. The rest of us looked nervously at Kenny, who hadn't turned a hair.

"She's really mad," Lyndz said in a low voice.

"Oh, she'll get over it," Kenny said easily. "She loves it, really, you know. Anyway, how about a game of Bed Frisbee?"

Bed Frisbee is one of Kenny's inventions, surprise surprise. One person bounces on the bed, while another throws a frisbee at them which the bed-person has to catch, still bouncing. It's really difficult, and you get so out of breath, it's dead hard to control what you're doing and catch the frisbee each time. It always ends with us collapsing in giggles on the bed, feeling all weak and silly.

To make it even harder, Kenny said we had to be in character for the game – so we each had to act as our pantomime character while we bounced up and down! It was just about impossible to keep a straight face, watching Fliss doing her woe-is-me routine in mid-air – even she got the giggles after a while. That became our sort of catchphrase for the evening, so each time someone missed the frisbee, everyone chorused, "Woe is YOU!" It's the sort of thing that Fliss could have got a bit stroppy about. After all, she does hate being teased by us, but she ended up having as much of a laugh as the rest of us did.

After we'd had our tea and watched a bit of TV, we all cleaned our teeth and got into our sleeping bags in a long line on the floor. As usual, we started discussing the pantomime.

"Who do you think will be Prince Charming?" Lyndz asked sleepily.

"Oh, I hope it's Ryan!" Fliss said at once. "That would be *soooo* wonderful!"

If you didn't know, Fliss has got a real crush on Ryan Scott at school. She's convinced she's going to marry him and everything, it's totally bizarre.

"Wouldn't it be romantic?" she continued. "Me as Cinderella, Ryan as Prince Charming! Oh, I hope I get to kiss him on stage!"

"*Fliss!*" Kenny said, laughing. "You're starting to sound like Molly!"

Just as she said the word "Molly", there was a soft popping sound from somewhere in the darkness.

"What was that?" I asked, and then one whiff of air told me. "Ugh! Gross!" It was a *stink bomb*!

Merry Christmas, Sleepover Club!

"Poo! Eeeeurrggggh!" we all said. "Quick, open the window!"

"I think I'm going to be sick!" Fliss groaned dramatically. "Ugh, that is totally disgusting!"

Kenny flung open the door and I pushed open her window, and we all breathed in the fresh air thankfully.

"Molly the Monster strikes again!" Kenny said grimly. "She's such a pig! Talk about Ugly Sisters – I know exactly who to imitate when I go for the audition!"

Fliss was hanging her head out of the window. "I hate your sister, Kenny," she moaned. "AND it's freezing out here!"

"It must be a warning from her, about not telling your mum and dad about her boyfriend," Lyndz said, holding her nose.

"Pah! It'll take more than a stink bomb to shut me up," Kenny said scornfully. "I've got plans for Saturday afternoon now, and her date with Mr Andy Pandy. Sabotage plans!"

CHAPTER FIVE

We didn't get to hear about Kenny's "sabotage plans" until Monday morning at school – but it was worth the wait.

Not only did she follow Molly into town on Saturday afternoon, but she hung around until Molly met Andrew ("who's a right nerd, by the way"), then snuck into the cinema after them and sat right behind them. Kenny told us that as soon as Andrew's arm started creeping around Molly's shoulders, Kenny tapped him on the shoulder.

"Excuse me, but as my sister's chaperone, I'd like to ask you to remove your arm from

Merry Christmas, Sleepover Club!

her," she whispered to him. "No hanky-panky on the first date!"

Well apparently, if looks could kill, Kenny would be six feet under by now. Molly went purple, tried to strangle Kenny – and then all three of them got chucked out of the cinema for fighting.

"You are *sooooo* evil!" Frankie said respectfully. "I'm totally glad I don't have a sister like you!"

"Serves her right for nearly suffocating us with that stink bomb," Kenny said airily. "I just WISH I'd thought to play that tape I made of Molly telling Carli about kissing him! Can you imagine how embarrassing THAT would have been?"

We all shook our heads at her. Kenny could be so horrible sometimes!

"Remind me never to get on the wrong side of you, Kenny," Lyndz said with a shudder.

"Anyway," Kenny continued, "they went off towards McDonald's after that – I tried to follow them but they gave me the slip. But Molly only went and told Mum what I'd done, and Mum went ballistic at me. She's stopped my pocket money for two weeks now."

"Gutted," I said sympathetically.

Kenny shrugged. "Oh, it was worth it!" she said. "I'd do it again for a month without pocket money, just to see the look on their faces! It was *soooo* funny!"

We were laughing so loudly, we didn't hear Mrs Weaver come in to do the register. She was carrying an armful of holly, which she started putting up around the classroom – a couple of sprigs above the blackboard and on the tops of the windows.

"There! Is everyone feeling Christmassy?" she said. "I hope so, because I've got some news for you. As well as the pantomime, we're going to be holding a Christmas bazaar this year to raise money for homeless people. Christmas isn't just about GETTING things, remember – it's about giving, too."

The classroom was silent as everyone listened closely.

"So in the next few weeks, we'll be making lots of things to sell at the bazaar, like calendars and Christmas stockings, and we're also asking parents to bake cakes and donate

Merry Christmas, Sleepover Club!

bric-a-brac for the stalls. And we'll be making a collection of food that we can give directly to the new homeless shelter in Leicester, so we're asking you to bring in tins of food, please – anything you can spare, so that some homeless people can have a nice Christmas dinner. Does everyone think that's a good idea?"

"Yes!" we all shouted.

"Good! Let's start this morning by making some calendars for the new year!" Mrs Weaver said. "There are lots of pieces of coloured card in the art cupboard plus glitter, paint, felt scraps – anything you like, to make it colourful and pretty. Just remember to leave a space at the bottom for your actual calendar, which is this big." She held one up to show everyone. "Other than that, you can let your imaginations go wild!"

I love making things at school. Mrs Weaver is quite arty-farty, so she always has wicked ideas for things we can do. We all got stuck into our calendars, and the morning flew by. Before we knew it, it was lunchtime – time for the auditions! EEEEK!!

The Sleepover Club

Lyndz was the only one of us five not to go along to Miss Middleton's classroom. She said there wasn't much point in her being there as she wouldn't have to audition to be a horse. It seemed like everyone else we knew was there, though. The M&Ms, Alana Banana, loads of boys from our class (including Ryan Scott, much to Fliss's delight). I suddenly started to feel a little bit nervous. Having to sing in front of all these people was going to be pretty scary!

Then I got a grip of myself. If I couldn't even sing in front of a few people from school, there was no way I'd EVER be able to sing in front of a huge audience, so it was just going to be a case of put up or shut up.

I took a few deep breaths and tried to think calming thoughts. The others all looked as petrified as me, apart from Kenny, who was doodling a fake Leicester City tattoo on her hand. Fliss was as white as a sheet.

"Thanks for coming, everyone," Miss Middleton said, clapping her hands for quiet. "This is the order we're going to do the auditions. Cinderella, Prince Charming,

Merry Christmas, Sleepover Club!

Wicked Wilma, Angelica, the narrator, Grizzle and Moana, and finally Buttons. When you audition for one part, you'll be considered for all the others, so you only need to give us one audition piece. We might think you're better suited to playing Angelica than Cinderella, for example, or Buttons rather than Prince Charming, so do have an open mind!"

Mrs Weaver stood up next. "As we're so short on space in here, once you've auditioned for a part, you're free to leave and go out into the playground with everyone else," she said. "Right! Can we have the Cinderellas first, please? Everyone else, sit back and be very quiet. And I'm sure I don't need to say this, but just in case – we don't want anyone sniggering or making silly remarks. Anyone who does so will have to leave the auditions, OK?"

"Yes," everyone muttered. I was secretly glad she'd said that, though. Imagine if you did your piece and the boys started making stupid comments. Embarrassing or WHAT?!

About fifteen of us went up to try out for the Cinderella role. My legs were starting to feel wobbly and my throat was all dry with nerves. I crossed my fingers, praying I wasn't about to make a great big chump of myself. I couldn't think of anything worse.

Miss Middleton passed around some sheets of the script. It was a scene between Cinderella and Prince Charming, and I scanned through it quickly, looking for any words I didn't know how to pronounce. It all looked quite easy, though.

"I feel sick," Fliss whispered to me. I gave her hand a squeeze, not wanting to admit how sick I was feeling, too.

"I'll read the part of Prince Charming," Miss Middleton said. "OK, who wants to go first? Felicity?"

Fliss stared at her, horrified. She looked like one of the rabbits you sometimes see on the road late at night, staring at car headlamps as if they're in a trance.

I gave her a nudge. "Break a leg!" I whispered.

She looked as if she'd been stung, and just stood there, still transfixed.

"Good luck!" I said, pushing her forward.

Merry Christmas, Sleepover Club!

Fliss stood opposite Miss Middleton at the front of the classroom. I could see that her hands were shaking terribly. Poor Fliss! Suddenly I felt really sorry for her, having to go first. This could be a bit painful to watch...

"Would you care for another dance?" said Miss Middleton, reading from the script.

There was a pause.

"I... I..." stammered Fliss, staring at the paper as if the script was written in a foreign language.

Someone tittered from the back of the classroom – it sounded like one of the M&Ms, but I couldn't be sure.

"OK, take a deep breath, let's start again," Miss Middleton said kindly. "Would you care for another dance?"

"I-I-I have to go," Fliss said in a tiny little voice. Her face had gone bright red. "I-i-i-it's almost m-m-m-midnight."

"But you still haven't told me your name!" Miss Middleton said.

"It's Fliss!" Fliss said in surprise. Hadn't Miss Middleton just called her Felicity a moment ago? Had she forgotten already?

69

There were a couple of laughs at that, and Fliss went even more red. "Oh, sorry," she said, looking down at the script, all flustered. Then she bit her lip. "I can't do this!" she wailed and ran out of the classroom.

The door banged shut behind her and everyone looked at each other.

"I can't do this!" Simon Graham said in a silly high voice, and all the boys started laughing their heads off.

"Any more noise from you lot and you'll be out on your ears!" Mrs Weaver said crossly. "Oh dear. We seem to have lost our first Cinderella. Lisa, would you like to read next?"

Lisa Warren stepped up opposite Miss Middleton. She'd only started at our school in September, and we didn't really know her as she was in Mr Nicholls' class. She was very pretty with long blonde hair, and as soon as she started reading, my heart did a sickening kind of lurch. She was good. No, she was better than good. She was REALLY good. She had a clear, confident speaking voice and seemed quite at ease in front of the classroom of people. Straight away, you believed in her, you believed she was really Cinderella.

Her singing voice was even better, I'm mega jealous to say. Miss Middleton asked her to sing *The First Noel*, and she sounded great. Got every high note, stayed in tune, the lot. By the time she'd finished, I knew I had a lot to live up to! Hmmm...

Emily Berryman went next. Her acting wasn't bad but her singing was terrible. She sang in a really high voice that wobbled all over the place, and she put on this yucky simpering expression as she sang. I mentally crossed her off the list. No way, José!

Then it was me. Gulp! I saw Frankie and Kenny giving me thumbs-up signs and big grins which made me feel a bit better, but my legs still wobbled a bit as I went up in front of everyone.

By now, I knew the scene pretty well, so at least I wasn't coming to it completely cold. I tried to speak as clearly as I could, but still managed to fluff a couple of words. I kept trying to imagine just what Cinderella would be feeling as the Prince begged her to stay for another dance. She would be feeling all happy and excited that the Prince seemed to like her, yet worried that if the clock struck midnight before she got home, her beautiful dress would turn into rags again, and her secret would be out.

It was all over before I knew it, and suddenly it was just me, Rosie, in the classroom again. And now I had to sing in front of everyone! I've never been keen on *The First Noel*, either. There are lots of really high bits and some quite low bits, too, so it's a real test of the old vocal chords. I was a bit shaky to begin with, but once I'd warmed up, I didn't think I'd done too badly. And that was it. Game over!

"Thank you, Rosie," said Mrs Weaver, smiling at me. "You can go off for your lunch now."

I was a bit gutted to have to leave so soon – I'd been hoping to see all the other auditions. I gave Frankie and Kenny a wave, just as Emma Hughes stepped up for her turn. Well, I'd given it my best shot, anyway. Let's hope the teachers thought it was OK, too!

I met up with Fliss and Lyndz in the

Merry Christmas, Sleepover Club!

playground, and then Frankie and Kenny joined us as soon as they'd finished.

"You missed a treat!" Kenny said gloatingly. "Emma Hughes really bodged it up in there! She was so hammy, it was hilarious! And her voice! What a croak! Oh, I wish you'd been there to see it. Me and Frankie were wetting ourselves!"

Fliss went pale. "Is everyone saying things like that about me?" she asked, practically in a whisper.

"Of course not!" Frankie said kindly. "It must have been horrible, having to go up there first, I would have hated it!"

Fliss scuffed her shoe on the ground. "It was Rosie's fault, anyway," she said in a cross little voice.

"Me? But why? What did I do?" I asked indignantly.

"You told me to break my leg!" she said accusingly. "I thought you were my friend, and then to tell me to break my leg just before I did my bit – I was very hurt!"

Kenny burst out laughing. "Fliss, what are you like?" she groaned.

73

"It's an expression they use in the theatre!" I said, losing my patience with Fliss. "It means good luck!"

"Never mind, Fliss," Lyndz said comfortingly. "Why don't you ask if you can be one of the horses with me?"

"No, thanks!" Fliss said rudely. "Who wants to be a smelly old horse?" And she stomped off in a huff.

"There's no pleasing some people," I said. "Let her stew. I'd feel a bit of an idiot, too, if I'd rushed out of there like she did."

"How were your auditions anyway?" Lyndz asked Frankie and Kenny.

"Pretty good!" Frankie said. "So many people went for Cinderella, there was only me and Alana Banana who went for the part of Wicked Wilma. And Alana went bright red and muttered all her words in this sort of monotone, so I don't think she stands much of a chance!"

"Likewise," said Kenny. "Can you believe, I was the only one who went for an Ugly Sister part?! Everyone else must be far too vain to want a part like that! And I made Mrs Weaver

Merry Christmas, Sleepover Club!

laugh at my reading, too, so..."

"Excellent!" I said. I was starting to worry that maybe I'd pushed my luck, going for such a major part. What if I wound up with big fat nothing?

Just then, a shout went up around the playground. "The cast list is up! The list is up!"

The four of us looked at each other.

"Already?" I said, feeling a bit faint. "That was quick!"

"Oh, per-leeeeze let me be an Ug!" Kenny said, breaking into a run towards the school hall. "Come on, let's check it out!"

CHAPTER SIX

As we ran back into school, I could feel my heart pounding. Please, please, let me be *something*, I wished inside my head. Even if it meant being an Ugly Sister, I was dying to have some part or other. Maybe it was horrible of me to feel glad about it, but I was relieved that at least I knew Fliss wouldn't be Cinderella. That was one less person in the running for it, anyway – and she would have been totally unbearable if she HAD got the part, more to the point!

There was quite a crowd around the noticeboard in the school hall. We pushed our way forward, trying to spot our names on the printed piece of paper. I looked desperately for mine next to the part of Cinderella, but then my shoulders slumped as I read the name. Lisa Warren. Well, she HAD been good – better than me, anyway. Still, it didn't make me feel any less disappointed.

"Yes!! Wicked Wilma – Frankie Thomas!" Frankie read aloud, punching the air and whooping. "RESULT!! Excellent, fantastic, I'm in the pantomime!"

Kenny had pushed her way right to the front. "So am I!" she yelled excitedly. "I'm down to play Grizzle! COOL!! I'm an Ug!"

I chuckled as I saw who was playing Moana. "Have you seen who they cast you with?" I asked, pointing at the name. "Look!"

Kenny read the paper eagerly, and then her face fell. "I don't believe it! Emma Hughes! Great – me and my bezzy mate, I don't think!" Then she paused. "Hey, actually, that's really funny, because she didn't even audition for that, did she? She auditioned for Cinderella! Ha ha!! She's going to be so mad when she sees that!"

Kenny scoured the hall for Emma. Ahh,

The Sleepover Club

there she was, rushing forward expectantly to see if she'd been given a part. Had she ever!

"Yoo-hoo!" Kenny yelled, waving madly at her. "Emma! You and me, mate! We're the Uglies!"

"Ha ha, very funny," Emma sneered, turning away from her and going up to the noticeboard.

"Oh dear, look at that, she doesn't even believe me!" Kenny sniggered. "Get used to the idea – it's me and you as the Ugly Twins!"

Emma clapped a hand over her mouth and looked really upset as she saw the truth for herself. For a moment, I actually felt sorry for her. Talk about a public humiliation!

I sighed, still feeling disappointed that I hadn't been picked. But there were only a handful of main parts after all, and maybe I could be in the chorus or something…

Then Lyndz was tugging my sleeve. "Hey, look, Rosie, here's your name!" she shouted. "You're Buttons!"

Buttons! I had a part! I stared at the cast list, unable to believe it was true. But there, in black and white, it said, "Buttons – Rosie

Merry Christmas, Sleepover Club!

Cartwright." So it WAS true!

"Yes!!" I screamed, jumping up and down in excitement. "I got a part!" I was SOOOO happy, I can't tell you! So I hadn't been picked for Cinderella, big deal! The teachers still thought I was good enough to be in the pantomime!

The full cast list went like this:

```
Cinderella - Lisa Warren
Prince Charming - Neil Watson
Narrator - Simon Graham
Wicked Wilma - Frankie Thomas
Angelica - Sarah King
Grizzle / Moana - Laura McKenzie
                / Emma Hughes
Buttons - Rosie Cartwright
```

Wow! I was *soooo* excited!

"It's a fix," I heard Emily Berryman muttering spitefully. "The crummy Sleep-tight Club have got THREE of the main parts. It's a total fix, if you ask me!"

"Judging will be on talent, not looks, as Mrs

Weaver said," Kenny told her sweetly. "Otherwise YOU probably would have got the part of Grizzle, not me!"

THAT shut her up!

There was a note at the bottom of the list:

```
Anyone interested in dancing,
singing or other non-speaking
parts, please come along to a
meeting in Miss Middleton's
classroom, Tuesday lunchtime.
First rehearsal - Thursday
lunchtime in the hall.
```

Thursday lunchtime! I could hardly wait!

I told my family about the whole thing over tea that night. My mum gave me a big hug and kiss. She's not normally the soppy type, but she kept telling me how proud of me she was. "My little girl on the stage, I can't believe it!" she kept saying.

"MU-U-U-UM!" I kept saying back.

"Well, we'll *all* be there in the audience!" she

said, ruffling my hair. "Fancy that, my little girl, eh!"

"You're in a good mood, Mum," Tiffany said. "Did you get a pay-rise at work or something?"

"Oh, that'll be the day," she said. "No, work's just... really good fun at the moment."

Me, Tiffany and Adam all stared at her in disbelief. Work – fun? Mum had never given us the impression that her office job was anything other than Dullsville Central. Even stranger than that, she started going a bit pink.

"Oh, you know, there's a good team of us at the moment, that's all," she said breezily. "Now eat your dinner before it gets cold!"

Tiffany raised her eyebrows and smirked. "I see!" she said. "And does this team have anything to do with that Richard guy you were talking to Auntie Zoë about?"

Mum blushed. I swear, my mum blushed like a teenager! Then she gave this mysterious smile. "You shouldn't listen to other people's conversations!" she said to Tiffany, wagging a finger at her. "You never know what trouble it's going to get you into!"

Tiffany gave her a knowing look, and I watched open-mouthed. Was Tiff saying what I thought she was? Was something going on with Mum and this Richard guy? For all my saying I wished Mum had a new boyfriend, I suddenly felt a bit worried about it. How did I know this Richard bloke would be good enough for her? What if he upset her, like Dad had done? Worst of all, what if WE didn't like him?

"Rosie, eat your mash, it's getting cold," Mum said. "And don't look so worried! Tiffany might think she knows everything, but she doesn't." She gave me a big wink and I felt a bit better. Still, I couldn't help wondering...

That week at school was really fun. Lyndz and Fliss went along to the auditions on Tuesday, and Lyndz duly got to be a horse, while Fliss got a part as a dancer in the ball scene, which she was really pleased about. "At least I don't have to say anything!" she said, smiling in relief. "AND I'll get to wear a nice dress!"

Emily Berryman still hadn't forgiven us for getting good parts when all she had got was a place in the choir – goodness only knows why, when her voice was so terrible. She was definitely miffed with us, AND with Lisa for getting the part of Cinderella.

"Everyone knows her dad's in prison," Emily said spitefully. "I can't believe a jailbird's daughter is going to be Cinderella. She's only been at this school for five minutes, too, it's not fair! And do you know what? Her family live on the council estate, too, you know that really horrible one, on Cuddington Road? Yeah, there! Don't go near her – she's probably got fleas!"

This all made me really mad. For starters, I used to live on a council estate a few years ago, and there was nothing wrong with it. Just because Emily lived in one of the big posh detached houses near Cuddington Park!

"You are such a snob, Berryman," I said. "AND you're jealous, just because Lisa was miles better than you in the audition! Don't spread lies about people when you don't know what you're talking about!"

"Ooh, since when did you become Lisa Warren's bodyguard?" Emily sneered. "Can't she stick up for herself?"

"I'm sure she can, but she's not here right now, is she?" I retaliated. "You're such a coward! You don't have the guts to say any of your nasty little remarks to her face, so you have to say it all behind her back!"

"Hear, hear," said Kenny. "So do us all a favour and shut up, Berry-head! Go and practise your crummy songs while WE learn our lines!"

Emily's lips were clamped shut so tightly, you couldn't have slid a piece of paper between them. She looked seriously hacked off now. Good, she deserved it!

Meanwhile, we carried on making things for the Christmas bazaar in lesson time, and people started bringing in bagloads of bric-a-brac to sell, plus food for the homeless shelter. Mrs Poole, the head teacher, set up a table in the hall to display all the food people had brought in, and the collection grew and grew. Soft-hearted Lyndz even brought in her chocolate Advent calendar to give to a homeless child. I told you she was the kindest person in the world, didn't I?

Merry Christmas, Sleepover Club!

Then came the first rehearsal for the pantomime! I'd been looking forward to it all week. I wasn't even quite sure how much Buttons had to say, so I was really dying to get a good look at the script so I could start thinking about how I'd say all my lines. I still couldn't believe that I, Rosie Cartwright, was going to be up on the stage in costume, acting in front of a big audience of parents and teachers and children. Every time I thought about it, I got butterflies. Scary!

The first thing Miss Middleton handed around was a rehearsal schedule. This gave the dates and times of each rehearsal, plus who had to be there for each one. Obviously Lisa, as Cinderella, had to go to nearly every one of them, as she was in most scenes. Frankie, Kenny and Emma also had quite a busy schedule. Mine wasn't too bad. I was in about four scenes by the look of it, so I wouldn't have to go to every single rehearsal. There were also separate rehearsals for all the dancers, and separate ones for the chorus. It was quite complicated, and I started to think that Miss Middleton deserved a medal for organising the whole thing!

Next, Miss Middleton handed round copies of the script to everyone who had speaking parts. At last! A chance to see what we would actually be saying! There were song sheets for the chorus to be passed round, too, and a more general scene-by-scene breakdown so people like Lyndz could see what scenes they were in. Soon, everyone was busily reading away with great interest.

Miss Middleton rapped on the desk after a minute or so. "OK!" she said. "I know you're all dying to read the scripts but there'll be plenty of time for that later. You'll notice that lots of rehearsals for the actors are after school, so please make sure your parents know where you are, and please also make sure you can get home safely afterwards. If anyone is really stuck for a lift, come and tell me or Mrs Weaver.

"Dancers and singers, you'll be rehearsing at lunchtimes mostly, although obviously there will be a few after-school rehearsals nearer the actual shows where everyone will rehearse together. If you go off with Mrs

Merry Christmas, Sleepover Club!

Weaver now, she'll tell you a bit more about it."

There was lots of kerfuffle as the dancers and singers all went off into the next classroom, Fliss included.

"Now, we don't have time to do very much today," Miss Middleton said to the rest of us, "but I thought we could begin by reading through the script together, just so you can start getting used to it. You don't have to stand up, just follow the script and read your lines out when you have them. So if you could all turn to the first scene, Simon, the narrator speaks first. When you're ready – let's go!"

Simon cleared his throat. "It was a cold December morning, and the De Vere family were eating breakfast together. Little did they know the postman was about to bring a letter that would change all of their lives."

Lisa spoke next, with Cinderella's first lines. "More coffee, madam? Can I get anyone some more toast?"

"This coffee is disgusting!" Frankie said, as Wicked Wilma. She said it so furiously, a couple of people giggled. "Honestly, Cinderella, is it too much to ask you to make a half-decent breakfast for your own stepmother?"

"AND the toast's cold," Kenny said as Grizzle, leering horribly. "Mama, Cinderella's just too lazy to make it properly!"

Then it was me! "The post has arrived, madam!" I said, and pretended to pass a bundle of letters to Frankie. "There's one letter with the royal crest on it!"

I felt myself go bright red after I'd spoken. Had I said it too fast? I glanced anxiously at Miss Middleton, who gave me a little wink.

"The royal crest? OOOH, I say!" said Frankie. More titters. I could tell she was really getting into the part!

"What is it, Mama?" said Emma, as Moana.

"Quick, open it, Mama!" said Kenny.

Frankie mimed tearing an envelope open and reading a letter. "Ooh, girls!" she said, fanning herself with her hand. "Ooh, you'll never guess! We've been invited to a BALL! Yes, a ball – with none other than Prince Charming himself there!"

"Prince Charming?" said Cinderella.

Wicked Wilma gave a horrible frown. "Yes,

Merry Christmas, Sleepover Club!

Cinderella, Prince Charming," she said. "Although why you're interested, I really don't know! YOU'RE certainly not invited to the ball! You'll be staying at home and cleaning out the kitchen cupboards!"

Miss Middleton clapped her hands. "Very good!" she said. "We're going to have to finish there, I'm afraid, as it's nearly time for lessons."

"Oh-h-h-h!" everyone said in disappointment. The time had flown by!

Miss Middleton smiled. "So take your scripts home and read through your lines over the weekend, won't you? First rehearsal proper is Monday night. Please make a note of all the rehearsals you're meant to be at, won't you? And I'll see some of you then!"

As everyone reluctantly left the room, the four of us grinned at each other.

"This is going to be FUN!" said Frankie happily.

I couldn't have put it better myself!

CHAPTER SEVEN

I couldn't believe it was Friday again already. It really is true that time flies when you're having fun. Already, there were only three weeks left until the end of term, and then it was Christmas itself!

Lyndz had organised the sleepover at hers for that night. She was calling it an early Christmas sleepover, and said she and her mum had made a load of mince pies for us to scoff. Yummo!

However, the spirit of giving and receiving didn't seem to have affected everyone at school. It seemed like someone had the spirit of TAKING instead.

Merry Christmas, Sleepover Club!

It was sharp-eyed Kenny who noticed something was wrong. Every Friday morning, different classes take it in turns to give a morning assembly in the hall on whatever topic they've been learning about recently. And after this week's, an incredibly boring one by Mrs Burgess's class about bears, we were just about to go to our classroom when Kenny pointed to the "food for the homeless" table.

"Look!" she said. "The Advent calendar you brought in has gone, Lyndz!"

We all stared. Sure enough, it had!

"It must be there SOMEWHERE," Lyndz said, scanning all the goodies that were piled up on the table. "It can't have just disappeared!"

"Unless someone's nicked it," I said thoughtfully. "Is everything else there?"

We went over to have a quick look.

"The stuff I brought in is all still there," Frankie said. "No, wait! Those chocolate biscuits Mum made me bring in have gone! And they were definitely on the table yesterday, because I remember being really gutted that she'd given them away."

"The tins of chickpeas I brought in are still there," Fliss said.

"You surprise me!" Kenny said sarcastically. "I'd have thought they would be the first things to be nicked!"

Fliss laughed. "I was glad to see them go, actually," she confessed. "They don't half make me... well, you know!"

"Beans, beans, good for your heart," I said. "The more you eat, you more you..."

"FART!" everyone joined in.

"Yes, exactly," Fliss said, blushing.

"So if anyone nicks the chickpeas, at least we know to look out for someone with a terrible wind problem," Frankie joked.

"I just can't believe someone is stealing stuff at all!" Lyndz said, as we went back to our classroom. "Stealing food that's meant to go to homeless people – I mean, how out of order can you get?"

"That sounds serious!" came Mrs Weaver's voice, who'd fallen into step behind us. "Stealing food? Who's been stealing food?"

"We don't know," I said. "But we just noticed that a couple of things we'd brought in for the homeless aren't on the table any more."

"Really?" Her face darkened. "Well, that IS serious. Thank you for telling me, girls."

Once in the classroom, we sat down at our desks, and Mrs Weaver rapped on the desk with a ruler to get everyone's attention. "Listen, please! I've just been informed that some of the food that was donated for the homeless shelter has disappeared," she said, frowning. "Obviously, if someone is stealing the food, this is a terrible thing to do. Every child at this school has a roof over their heads and is well fed. To think that someone could be taking food that is meant to go to people who have nowhere to live... Well, it's extremely disappointing to think that someone could do such a thing."

Everyone looked at their desks in silence. Mrs Weaver has this way of making you feel bad about something even if you haven't done anything wrong.

"I bet you it's Lisa Warren," Emily Berryman said in a loud whisper.

"Emily, do you have something to say to the class?" Mrs Weaver asked in an icy voice.

Emily looked crestfallen. "No, Miss," she muttered.

"Good," said Mrs Weaver. "Because stealing food is one thing. Spreading rumours about who's responsible for it is almost as despicable. So if I find out that anyone is gossiping or making allegations, I will be extremely angry – especially if that someone is in my class!"

I snuck a quick look at Emily, who looked utterly embarrassed. Good! I thought. She was asking for it, coming out with comments like that about Lisa.

Unfortunately, the M&Ms don't give up that easily with their nastiness. By playtime, it was all over the school that Lisa and her little brother Michael had been taking the food because their family couldn't afford to buy any. You know what it's like when a rumour starts at school. It was all anyone could talk about – Cinderella the thief!

I felt really sorry for Lisa. Well, we all did. No-one deserved to be judged like that, without any proof. Whatever happened to "innocent until proven guilty", anyway?

Merry Christmas, Sleepover Club!

The five of us went over to Lisa, who was sitting on a wall, all on her own. She looked really miserable.

"Just ignore what everyone's saying," Lyndz said hotly, putting an arm around her. "WE know it wasn't you that nicked the food."

"Everyone's just jealous because you're going to be a great Cinderella," Frankie said. "Stupid idiots! Lyndz is right."

Lisa's eyes were red as she forced a smile. "I know you're right," she said, "but it's horrible to have the whole school talking about you. And until they find out who's REALLY taking the food..." She shrugged miserably, and didn't bother to finish her sentence.

I caught Kenny's eye. "Maybe we should try and catch the thief," I suggested. "Then we could get you off the hook, and everyone would leave you alone."

"Mmm," said Lisa, although she didn't sound convinced. "Thanks, you lot. I need all the friends I can get right now."

"You just leave it to us," Kenny said confidently. "We'll sort it out! Sleepover Club to the rescue!"

The Sleepover Club

* * *

That night at the sleepover, we started wondering if we'd been a bit rash, promising to clear Lisa's name like that.

"It's a good idea, but HOW are we going to catch the thief?" I said, racking my brains.

"And are we sure Lisa *didn't* take the food, anyway?" Fliss sniffed. "After all, she *is* poor, isn't she?"

We all stared at her, horrified.

"Fliss!" Kenny said fiercely. "I didn't think YOU were like all the others! Don't be so horrible!"

"I can't believe you just said that, Fliss," Lyndz said, looking really shocked. "Being poor doesn't make someone a thief. Look at all those rich businessmen and politicians who swindle thousands of pounds out of other people!"

"And so what if her family IS a bit hard up, anyway?" I said. "You can't judge a person on their *money*!"

Fliss looked a bit shaken at our angry words. "S-sorry," she stammered in the end. "I just..."

"You've got a problem with her, just because she's Cinderella," Frankie said sharply. "Well, get over it!"

There was a bit of an awkward silence. Lyndz handed round the plate of mince pies and we all munched away. Honestly, Fliss doesn't half come out with stupid comments sometimes.

"Maybe we should set a trap for the thief," Fliss suggested in the end. You could tell she was trying to make up for what she'd said about Lisa. "Maybe we could rig up a booby trap or something..."

"My brother's got some of this marking powder that looks invisible, but when you touch something with the powder on, it turns your hands black," Lyndz said excitedly. "We could cover all the food with the powder, and then just keep an eye on everyone's hands! It takes days for the colour to fade!"

"What if the powder poisons the food?" I pointed out. "Besides, there's loads and loads of food to cover with this powder, we'd need tons of it."

"And there's new stuff going on the table

every day," Kenny added. "It would be a nightmare, trying to keep track of what we'd powdered and what we hadn't."

Lyndz's face fell in disappointment.

"Good idea, though," Frankie said kindly.

We all thought a bit more.

"How about putting a banana skin under the table so that the thief skids on it, falls over, bashes their head on the edge of the table and knocks themselves out?" Kenny joked.

"Yeah, or build a trap door under the table that they'd fall through, straight into a steel cage?" I said, giggling.

"Or one of us could hide under the table and grab their legs and rugby-tackle them when they came up to nick something!" Frankie said. "Biff! Gotcha, my son!"

We all started thinking of more and more ridiculous ideas to catch the thief until we were all weak with giggles. Lyndz had just come up with a plan to rig up CCTV so that we could monitor the table at all times, when Kenny whistled excitedly.

"Hey! WE could be the CCTV!" she said.

We all stared at her blankly.

Merry Christmas, Sleepover Club!

"More, please," Frankie ordered. "We don't understand Kenny language!"

"We don't need CCTV to keep watch on the table, *we* can do it!" she laughed. "It's so simple, I can't believe we didn't think of it before! You know the music cupboard at the back of the hall where all the instruments are kept?"

"Ye-e-e-e-s," we chorused.

"Remember Mrs Weaver sent me and Alana Banana to put away the musical instruments last week?" she said, eyes sparkling. "Well, I just so happened to notice that the lock was broken. You can't tell from looking at it, but you don't need the key to open the door. So unless Dishy Dave has got round to fixing it super-quickly..."

"We can hide in the cupboard and spy out on the table!" I finished for her.

"Exactly!" she beamed. "What do you think?"

"We're not allowed inside at breaktimes," Fliss reminded us, shaking her head doubtfully.

Frankie rolled her eyes. "And? Your point

is?" she demanded. "Since when have a few rules stopped the Sleepover Club?"

"It's definitely worth a try," Lyndz said. "The only thing is, for us to catch the thief, they have to nick stuff at breaktimes. I mean, I don't really want to be hanging around *after* school in the music cupboard..."

"Think about it!" Kenny said. "There'll be all the pantomime rehearsals and stuff after school anyway, so the hall's going to be out of bounds for the thief then. So if they're going to nick anything else, they'll have to do it before school starts or at lunchtime or playtime. And we'll make sure that WE'RE there to catch them when they next try it!"

"Kenny, you're a genius," I told her. "What would we do without you?"

"Oh, get very bored and miserable, I should think!" Kenny said, grinning. "So are we all agreed, then?"

"Agreed!" we all said together. Even Fliss!

Back at home, my mum's mysterious behaviour was continuing. She hummed whenever she was in the kitchen, smiled at herself when she passed any mirrors and spent AGES on the phone to my Auntie Zoë. Something was *definitely* up! The question was, WHAT?

That Saturday, she took me into Leicester for some Christmas shopping. Tiffany was out at a friend's house and Adam was over at my dad's, so it was just me and Mum for a change. I hardly ever get her to myself, so it always feels like a real treat when the two of us spend a bit of time together. Once again, she seemed really happy and kept laughing and joking about things, even when we were stuck in mile-long queues at the till. What was it all about?

In the end, the suspense was just way too much for me. I waited until we were having a cup of tea in a café, and then came straight out with it.

"Mum, something's going on, isn't it?" I said. No beating about the bush from Rosie!

She took a sip of her coffee. "What do you mean?" she asked.

"It's just... well, you seem different," I said, not quite sure how to put it into words.

The Sleepover Club

"Happier. I keep wondering about what Tiffany said the other day about Richard, your friend at work. I mean... is something going on?"

She put down her cup. "Well..." she said thoughtfully, "something MIGHT be about to go on. I really like Richard. He's been a very good friend to me. But my family are what's most important to me – you, Adam and Tiff. I'd only let anything happen with Richard if you three were OK with the idea. I mean, after your dad leaving us and everything..."

She shrugged, and then gazed down into her coffee. I slurped my Coke while I tried to work out how I felt about it. Sure, I'd hoped for ages that she and Dad would get back together. Who wouldn't? But Dad had his new family to think about, and deep down in my heart, I knew that he probably wouldn't be coming back to us.

"Go for it, Mum!" I said in the end. "I think you should just go for it with Richard! If he makes you happy, why not?"

She leaned over the table and hugged me. She looked all excited and girlish at the thought. "If you're sure you're OK with it?" she

Merry Christmas, Sleepover Club!

said again. "Only he's asked me to go to dinner with him next week and I said I'd ask you three first, so..."

"So go!" I said, smiling at her. I felt as if I was the parent suddenly, giving her permission to go out. "Cinderella, you SHALL go to the ball!"

CHAPTER EIGHT

The next week, pantomime rehearsals started in earnest. They were so much fun! As Buttons, I didn't have too many lines to learn, so I was quite relaxed about the whole thing and could sit back and enjoy watching the others.

Everyone else was having a good time, too. Kenny really got into her role as Grizzle and hammed it up a treat every time she was in a scene. She was determined to get more laughs than Emma's Moana, so she worked dead hard to make herself extra funny. Kenny's got one of those really mobile faces and is excellent at pulling comic expressions. After a while, she would have the whole cast roaring with laughter with the twitch of an eyebrow, or just by rolling her eyes up to the heavens.

Frankie was also loving it. Frankie's got an amazing brain for detail, and she'd memorised all her lines by the first rehearsal, so Miss Middleton was dead impressed with that. Frankie and Kenny played well off each other, too, so when they were both in the same scene, everyone would be chuckling away at them, even Miss Middleton and Mrs Weaver! Like Kenny, Frankie was a bit of a star in the making.

Right from the first rehearsal, though, it was Lisa who shone out as having a real acting talent. I actually began to feel glad that she'd got the part of Cinderella, and not me. She was head and shoulders above everyone else who was there, and I was chuffed for her, after all the horrible rumours that had been going around. Often after she'd rehearsed a scene, or one of her songs, I caught Miss Middleton and Mrs Weaver smiling away at each other, both looking dead pleased with their Cinders.

The only character who didn't seem that brilliant was Sarah King, the fairy godmother. She spoke clearly enough, but she was having terrible trouble learning her lines, even the most simple sentences.

I'm not saying I've got a fantastic memory or anything, but after hearing a scene rehearsed once or twice through, I found that even *I* knew her words, without even trying. It was *painful* to watch Sarah biting her lip, trying to think of what she had to say next.

"But Cinderella, you must promise me one thing," she was supposed to say in her first scene. "You must be back by the last stroke of midnight – for that's when the magic will vanish, and so will your dress, coach and horses!"

Sarah kept saying, "Cinderella, you must TELL me one thing" by mistake, which changed the meaning of the sentence completely. She just couldn't remember the word "promise" for the life of her.

"From the top," Miss Middleton called out patiently, and Lisa and Sarah began the scene again.

Merry Christmas, Sleepover Club!

"Don't look so..." Sarah started, then bit her lip anxiously. "Don't look so..."

"Frightened," I said, and then jumped at the sound of my own voice. Oops! I hadn't meant to say anything, it had just popped out of my mouth!

Sarah shot me a thankful look, and started again. "Don't look so frightened," she said, sounding more confident. "I'm your fairy godmother – and I'm here to help you, Cinderella!"

The next few lines went OK, with Lisa giving a faultless reading of Cinderella and Sarah managing to remember all her words. Then it came to the "promise" line, and...

"Cinderella, you must tell me one thing," Sarah said.

"Promise me," I said. Again, I just couldn't stop myself saying it! I didn't want to butt in or anything, but I couldn't help feeling a bit sorry for Sarah struggling up there on the stage.

She smiled gratefully at me again. "Cinderella, you must PROMISE me one thing," she said, turning back to Lisa. "You must be back by the last stroke of midnight..."

The Sleepover Club

I was a bit worried that Miss Middleton might think I was poking my nose in where it wasn't wanted. And sure enough, at the end of that night's rehearsal, she and Mrs Weaver called me over to them. Uh-oh! I was going to get told to keep my mouth shut when I wasn't involved in rehearsals!

"There's no need to look like that, you're not in trouble!" Mrs Weaver laughed as I came over. "Dear me, you look like a wet weekend, Rosie!"

I smiled weakly at her, wondering what this could be all about. "I'm sorry I told Sarah her lines," I said quickly, thinking that if I could get an apology in first, they might not be cross with me.

"That's what we wanted to talk to you about," Miss Middleton said. "We realised what's missing from our rehearsals – a couple of prompts! Obviously we'll be busy directing the actors so won't always have a script to hand..."

".... But as you seem to be picking the lines up pretty quickly, we wondered if you'd like to sit in as one of the prompts, when you're not rehearsing your scenes?" Mrs Weaver asked.

"What's a prompt?" I asked, feeling a bit stupid. Well, I didn't know!

"A prompt basically does what you did tonight," Miss Middleton said. "They sit by the side of the stage and when someone forgets their lines, the prompt reminds them of the next couple of words. Think you could do that?"

I grinned from ear to ear. "Yes! Oh, yes, definitely! I'm sure I could!" I said, feeling utterly delighted. Anything to get more involved in the play!

"It would mean coming to more rehearsals," Mrs Weaver said. "Would that be a problem?"

"No! No! That's fine!" I said happily. Buttons AND a prompt! This was getting better and better.

"Good!" smiled Miss Middleton. "Thank you very much, Rosie! That will be a big help to us. Alex McKay will be our other prompt, so between you, I'm sure you'll do a great job."

Of the other two, Lyndz was enjoying being a horse, even though she didn't have to do very much. Still, that suited her, she said. No problem! It just meant she had more time to be off riding and mucking out REAL horses, in fact.

Fliss was getting into the dancing thing, too, and kept showing us her moves in the playground, twirling around all over the place until the rest of us were in fits of giggles.

"Wait until you see my dress!" she boasted. "It's really beautiful! Mrs Somersby said she's designing it especially for me, you know!"

"Funnily enough, she's designing MY costume especially for ME!" Frankie said dryly. "Strange that, isn't it, seeing as it's going to be me who's wearing it!"

"Oh, you know what I mean!" Fliss said, tossing her hair. "She said she wanted to make the most of my colouring and that. So there!"

The only thing Fliss DIDN'T like was when me, Frankie and Kenny talked about our rehearsals – or worse still, talked about how good Lisa was.

"When she sang that song today, I honestly got a lump in my throat," I told the others. "She really has got a fab voice!"

"And I love that first scene I do with her," Frankie said. "The one where I'm telling her she can't go to the ball and she's all miserable about it. Do you know, the other night, I was actually worried I'd really upset her because she seemed so gutted. But it was only because she was acting so brilliantly!"

"Oh, anyone can act if they want to," Fliss would sniff, turning her nose up a bit. "The thing is, who can be bothered? I'd much rather be a model any day."

"Proudlove, the green-eyed monster..." Kenny would sing under her breath to the tune of *Rudolf the Red-Nosed Reindeer*, or one of us would start humming the tune when Fliss started on her jealous routine. It wasn't worth falling out about, but it did get a bit annoying. I REALLY had to bite my tongue to stop myself reminding her about her audition disaster!

As well as the pantomime, we also made a start on Operation Food Nicker, as Frankie called it. Who had been helping themselves to the donated food – and why were they doing such a mean thing?

To be honest, it was pretty boring at first, especially as we'd half expected to catch the thief straight away and be done with it. I'd thought it might be quite an adventure, playing detective – but boy, was I wrong about THAT.

We took it in turns to hide in the cupboard in twos at lunchtimes and breaktimes, spying out on the food table. The first time I did it with Lyndz, it actually WAS quite exciting, as we were both convinced we would catch someone. Every time we saw someone walk anywhere near the table, we'd hold our breath and clutch each other, watching carefully to see if they'd stash anything in a bag or their pockets.

"OK, here we go," one of us would say. "Get ready to pounce!"

But no! It was just one false alarm after another. The nearest thing we got to a thief was when a woman we didn't recognise strolled right up to the table and started picking up tins and looking at them. Lyndz and I stared wide-eyed at each other. Talk about blatant! This was one confident thief, all right!

Merry Christmas, Sleepover Club!

But just as we were about to go out and make an accusation, who should walk up at that moment but Mrs Poole! "Yes, this is our collection of food for the homeless," she started saying to the mysterious woman.

Lyndz put a hand over her mouth to try and stop herself giggling. "You know who that is, don't you?" she spluttered.

"No," I said blankly.

"It's the new supply teacher!" she said. "And we were just about to...!"

So apart from that little near miss, the whole thing was a bit tedious. But the rumours were still flying about Lisa and Michael, and whenever I saw Lisa's anxious, pale face or heard the M&Ms gossiping loudly about her, I knew we had to do SOMETHING, however boring Operation Food Nicker was turning out to be.

Kenny insisted on it, anyway. "If someone's desperate enough to steal food, a warning from Mrs Poole won't stop them, will it?" she pointed out. "Whose turn is it this playtime? Me and you, Fliss, isn't it? Right! Come on, then!" And so we carried on with our mission...

Meanwhile, back at home, Mum had broken the news about this Richard guy to Tiffany and Adam, and they were both pleased for her. The date was on!

"The only trouble is," she confided in me and Tiff, "I've got absolutely nothing nice to wear."

It was true. Ever since Dad left, money's been a bit tight in our house, and what with Christmas coming up, Mum had no spare cash to buy a new outfit. Tiffany and I had a look through her wardrobe with her, but it was no good. Everything was old and faded and had been worn a hundred times before.

"I wonder if you could fit into anything of mine?" Tiff said to her in the end. "I mean, we're both about the same size, aren't we?"

Mum laughed. "Thanks, love, but I don't think I've got the legs for any of your little skirts these days," she said. "No, I'll just wear this black dress. It's the best of the bunch, isn't it?"

Well, it WAS the best of them, but it still looked pretty ancient, if you asked me. You know after you wash a pair of black trousers so many times, the black starts to look a bit grey? Well, this dress was grey, dowdy, and looked a hundred years old.

"Mum," I said tentatively, "I could ask Fliss's mum if you can borrow one of her dresses if you like. She's got loads."

My mum frowned at that. She's dead proud, and hates the idea of having to take anything from other people. "We're not a charity, Rosie," she said lightly, but I could tell she hated my offer. "No, the black dress will be fine!"

I felt bad for suggesting it, then, and sloped off to my room. I couldn't help thinking about Cinderella. What Mum really needed was a fairy godmother of her very own, to wave a magic wand and produce a gorgeous outfit out of thin air. But there was no such thing as fairy godmothers. Or was there?

I waited until Mum was in the bath that night, and Tiff and Adam were both watching telly. Then I picked up the phone and started dialling. You never knew – maybe I could work a bit of Christmas magic myself!

CHAPTER NINE

The next exciting thing to happen at school was that we caught the thief red-handed! Another storming success for the Sleepover sleuths!

The only thing was, it wasn't quite the triumph we'd all been expecting. I'd been convinced that the thief had to be someone really horrible and mean – I was even wondering if it was the M&Ms, trying to frame Lisa, to be honest.

Me and Frankie were keeping watch that breaktime. Well, I say "keeping watch", but we were so bored, we were actually playing noughts and crosses in the dust on the top of the piano. Frankie was sitting nearest the door, keeping half an eye out on the hall. I was too interested in the game to be paying any attention to the hall, or listening out for footsteps.

It was quite lucky that we caught him, all in all! Frankie had just trounced me, and leaned back to peep through the glass – and then nearly fell over in shock. She put a finger to her lips and motioned me to come forward. Then she pointed towards the food table.

There was a small figure, quickly tucking things into a small satchel for all he was worth. Frankie crashed through the door and sprinted over to him.

"Got you!" she yelled, grabbing hold of him.

I raced behind her, only to see that it was Andy Mitchell, one of the little Year Threes, looking absolutely petrified.

"Right – straight to Mrs Poole's with YOU!" Frankie said, marching him along by the scruff of his neck. "I think you've got some explaining to do, mate!"

Andy started to cry great snivelling sobs. "Please don't tell her," he wailed. "Please don't tell Mrs Poole!" He looked really scared at the mention of her name.

"But that food was for homeless people!" I said. "It's wrong to take it! That was supposed to be for their Christmas dinner!"

"I know," he blubbed. "I'm sorry. But..." He wiped his nose on his sleeve and we couldn't catch the rest of what he was trying to say, as his voice went all choky.

I have to say, I was starting to feel a teeny bit sorry for him. He was only a little kid, after all. Still, thieving was thieving, wasn't it?

"Oh dear," said Mrs Poole, when we walked into her office, Frankie and me on either side of Andy. "What have we here? What's going on?"

"We caught HIM stealing THIS," Frankie said triumphantly, holding the satchel of food up in the air. "He was at the food table, helping himself!"

"Is this true, Andy?" Mrs Poole said gently.

Andy nodded, keeping his eyes on the floor.

Mrs Poole handed him a tissue. "Blow your nose," she told him. "Now, what's all this about, then?"

Merry Christmas, Sleepover Club!

Andy blew his nose with trembling hands. "I know the food was meant for homeless people, Miss," he said, "but I was only trying to help my dad. He's lost his job and my mum says..." The rest of his sentence was lost in a new burst of sobs. "I'm s-s-so s-s-sorry," he wailed, blowing his nose again.

Frankie and I looked at each other. Suddenly I felt awkward. I wished the thief was an out-and-out villain that we could have despised. The fact that it was this poor little kid whose family were probably going to have a rotten Christmas... I didn't quite know how to feel about it any more.

Mrs Poole told Andy to sit down, then looked up at us two. "You can go," she said quietly. "Thank you for bringing this to my attention. I'd appreciate it if this could go no further."

"Yes, Miss," I said, anxious to get out of there.

"But what about Lisa and Michael?" Frankie blurted out. "Everyone's saying it's them!"

Mrs Poole thought for a few seconds. "I'll make sure everyone knows they had nothing to do with this," she said. "Thank you, girls."

Boy, was I glad to get out of that office. We rushed off to find the others straight away. Sure, Mrs Poole had said not to tell anyone, but we just HAD to tell the rest of the Sleepover Club, didn't we?

Kenny was jubilant. "What did I say? I just knew we had to stick at it!" she crowed. "Another result for us!"

"So who was it, anyway?" Lyndz said.

"Well..." I started, feeling a bit miserable about the whole thing. "It was this little lad Andy in Year Three. Turns out his dad's just lost his job. I think he was just trying to help out, you know."

Lyndz looked sympathetic, but Fliss wasn't. "Well! He can't just go around stealing like that, can he?" she said, sounding outraged.

"He's only about seven," Frankie pointed out. "And he was really sorry about it, wasn't he, Rosie?"

"Yeah," I said, thinking back to his tear-stained face. "He was crying his eyes out. I don't reckon HIS family are going to have a very nice Christmas this year."

We all went a bit quiet. We should have been feeling dead pleased with ourselves for catching him stealing, but none of us were.

"At least Lisa's off the hook," Kenny said brightly.

"Yeah," said Frankie. "That's true. Mrs Poole wants us to keep schtum about Andy, but she said she'd make sure everyone knew it WASN'T Lisa. So everyone keep their mouths shut, yeah?"

"Yeah," we all agreed. "Definitely."

Mrs Poole was as good as her word. The very next day at assembly, she stood up to make an announcement.

"I just want to say a big thank you to everyone who has brought in food for our homeless table," she started. "You've all been very generous, and I know the homeless centre will really appreciate what you've done for them. Thank you!"

Then she paused and looked serious. "Now, I'm sure you've all heard that some of the food was going missing, which we were very concerned about," she said. "And if this has made you think twice about bringing any donations in, then you'll be pleased to hear that the person responsible has been caught."

Lots of people started whispering to each other at this news. Mrs Poole clapped her hands for quiet.

"Listen, please!" she called. "Now, it's been brought to my attention that a couple of people have been spreading very nasty rumours about who the thief could be. I was very disappointed to hear this, as I had hoped all the children at my school would be fairer and more open-minded than that."

I shot a quick look at the M&Ms. They had both gone purple with embarrassment.

"Now, when someone's spreading rumours about you, it can be very hurtful and upsetting," Mrs Poole continued. "Obviously I'm not going to tell you all who the thief was, but I would like to make it clear that it was NOT Lisa Warren or her brother Michael – and anyone who has been saying otherwise should be very ashamed of themselves. I think a few people in this room owe Lisa and Michael an apology, don't you?"

Everyone was craning their necks to look at

Lisa and Michael. Lisa was bright red, too, but she was also looking relieved, and holding her head high as everyone stared.

"And finally," Mrs Poole went on, "a reminder that the Christmas bazaar is this Saturday, so I hope to see lots of you there. There are some fantastic prizes in the raffle so make sure you get tickets from your class teacher or, of course, at the bazaar itself."

"Oh, I hope I win the raffle!" Fliss said fervently, crossing her fingers. "There's this gorgeous nail varnish collection that I would die for!"

Mrs Burgess started playing *All Things Bright and Beautiful* on the piano just then so we had to stop talking and start singing. And suddenly… I know it sounds corny, but I was feeling really bright and beautiful myself. We'd cleared Lisa's name, the bazaar and pantomime were coming up, my mum was in lurve, and best of all, it was almost Christmas. Could life get any better?

Life DID suddenly get a lot better for my mum that week. My Auntie Zoë came round with a bag of goodies for her, as we'd arranged on the phone. Yes, this was Mum's real-life fairy godmother, come to the rescue on an emergency clothes mission!

I'd told Zoë the whole story about Mum not having anything nice to wear for her date with Richard, and she'd promised to try and help. The thing was, I'd told her she'd have to be really subtle about it. If Mum got a whiff of "charity", she'd refuse to take anything off her, and we'd be back to square one.

True to her word, Zoë arrived with a bulging carrier bag and a bottle of white wine. "Sandra next door is having a bit of a clear-out," she told Mum with a beaming smile. "So I've nabbed a whole load of stuff for us, Karen! I thought we could fight for it all over a few glasses of vino, what do you think?"

Tiffany immediately wandered over. "Ooh, can have second dibs on that lot, Auntie Zoë?" she asked, trying to peer in the bag. "I need something nice for my Christmas party at school."

"Oh no you don't!" Mum said at once. She took out two wine glasses and plonked them down on the table. "Zoë, you're an angel!" she said, smiling. Then a thought struck her. "Ooh – there might even be something in here that I can wear for my date with Richard!"

Zoë gave me the tiniest of winks as Mum started rummaging excitedly through the bag of clothes. "Oh, so that's all definitely going ahead then, is it?" Zoë asked casually. "Where's he taking you?"

"A new French restaurant in Leicester," Mum said happily.

You know, when my mum smiles and stops looking worried for five seconds, she actually looks really pretty. And just at that moment, she looked gorgeous! If this Richard guy had any sense, he'd fall head over heels in love with her – and one of my Christmas wishes would come true!

I grinned to myself as I left them to it. Yippee! It looked like fairy godmother Zoë was going to work her magic, just as I'd hoped she would.

Sure enough, when I casually wandered back into the living room an hour later, Mum and Zoë were sitting there in completely different outfits, giggling like schoolgirls about something or other, with about two centimetres of wine left in the bottle.

"Wow, Mum, you look nice!" I said. "Stand up, let's have a look!"

She stood up – a bit wobbly on her feet – and did a twirl for me. Good old Zoë had come up trumps. Mum had on another black dress, but it was a far cry from the old one she usually wore. This one looked almost new, and fitted her perfectly. The material was a soft jersey, so it clung in all the right places. She looked so good, even Fliss would have approved.

"Mum, that's gorgeous!" I said in delight. "You look really lovely!"

"Doesn't she?" Zoë agreed. "You're going to knock this new fella for six, Karen!"

Mum looked all embarrassed. "Stop it, you two!" she said, but I could tell she was pleased, really. "I must pop in and thank Sandra next time I'm over at yours, Zoë," she said. "Fancy wanting to get rid of this lovely dress!"

As Mum went out to make coffee, I moved

closer to Zoë. "Where did it really come from?" I asked in a low voice.

"From the seconds shop in Cuddington Road," she whispered back, tapping her nose. "But that's just between you and me. Mum's the word, eh?"

"Well, you'd better stop her nipping round to thank Sandra, then, hadn't you?" I said, giving her a hug. "Thank you!"

Mum came back in with a tray of coffee just then, followed by Adam in his wheelchair. I sniggered to see Adam's eyes goggling as he caught sight of Mum in her new dress.

He tried to wolf-whistle, but he's got this computerised voice box because of his cerebral palsy and his whistle came out as a sort of bleeping noise instead. Bleep-BLEEP! That just set me off giggling even more. It was such a funny noise, even Mum and Zoë joined in. Adam grinned and made the noise again and again until we were all roaring with laughter. Bleep-BLEEP! It made me feel all tingly inside with happiness. This was turning out to be a great month!

CHAPTER TEN

So that was my mum sorted, anyway! It was brilliant to see her so happy. If your parents are together, then you probably don't worry about them much, but if your parents are separated, like mine, you can't help it sometimes.

I don't want to sound like an old misery-guts and do a "woe is me" routine, especially just before Christmas, but it makes such a difference to your own life if your folks aren't happy. So now, every time I heard Mum singing in the shower, I felt this lovely warm feeling in my tummy. The magic of Christmas again!

Merry Christmas, Sleepover Club!

While Mum went on her date on Saturday night, I was busy at the school bazaar. Mrs Weaver had asked for volunteers to help run the stalls – so of course the Sleepover Club wanted to get involved somewhere or other. Lyndz wanted to help out on the cake stall (she's got a real sweet tooth!) but Fliss was worried about putting on weight before Christmas and ruled it out. So we got to help out on the raffle instead.

Of course, the worst thing about doing that was that we had to sit staring at loads of fantastic prizes all night. A few local companies had donated stuff – so there was Fliss's beloved nail varnish collection donated by a cosmetics firm, a food hamper from one of the department stores in town, a lawnmower and some gift vouchers from the big DIY centre outside Leicester – and best of all, a mountain bike from Sports Warehouse. There were lots of other smaller prizes, too, like bottles of wine and chocolates, and even a voucher for a free facial at Curlers Beauty Parlour!

Every now and then, a couple of teachers

would come and relieve us so that we could go round the bazaar ourselves. It was excellent! Frankie won a wonky-eyed teddy on the hoopla, Fliss snapped up a beaded handbag for 20p on the white elephant stall, me and Lyndz splashed out on a couple of chocolate brownies each (well, selling raffle tickets was hungry work) and then Kenny went in for the netball challenge and won... a pair of sports socks!

At the end of the night, Mrs Poole started up the PA system and did the draw for the prizes. Fliss had bought so many tickets, her new handbag was practically full of them.

"And the winner of the Beauty Parlour facial is... number 280," Mrs Poole began.

We all looked around to see who'd won it. Simon Graham! He was so embarrassed, he tried to get his mum to go up and claim the prize for him, but she was laughing so much that he had to do it. Gutted!! Of course, we all wolf-whistled at him like mad!

After all her finger-crossing and ticket-buying, Fliss didn't win the nail varnish. "Number 530," Mrs Poole called out. Fliss's face when she hadn't got the ticket was a *picture*. She actually stamped her foot in temper!

But the person who DID have number 530 was Lisa – which I thought was really nice. Fliss wasn't so impressed, though.

"Typical!" she moaned. "First she steals my part in the pantomime, then she gets her mitts on my nail varnish!"

I was crossing my fingers like anything for the mountain bike. The bike I've got at the moment is a right old cronk, and I'd love to get a brand new one. Well, I didn't get it, but you'll never guess who won it instead! Little Andy Mitchell had the winning ticket – and you should have seen his face!

I caught Frankie's eye. "All's well that ends well," I said softly. It was amazing how this raffle was working out so perfectly.

None of us five won anything after all that, but I didn't really mind. The M&Ms would only have accused us of rigging it, anyway.

At the end of the night, Mrs Poole switched the PA system on again and took the microphone.

"Ladies and gentlemen, may I just have your attention for a few moments," she said. "Obviously we haven't done a final count-up of tonight's takings, but we've estimated the money you've all helped us to raise – and it looks like it'll be about five hundred pounds!"

A huge cheer went around the hall. Five hundred pounds! That was awesome!

"Thank you so much for your generosity," she went on. "This money will really make a difference to a lot of people this Christmas. Well done, everyone!"

When I got home that night, Mum still wasn't back, so the babysitter let me in. Me and Tiffany sat up late, pretending to write Christmas cards, but really so we could find out how Mum had got on when she came home.

It was just after midnight when we heard a car pull up outside. "Just like Cinderella!" I said, grinning. Tiff crossed her fingers excitedly as we heard the key turn in the lock.

"See you on Monday! Thanks for a lovely evening! Bye!" we heard Mum calling.

Merry Christmas, Sleepover Club!

She took one look at our faces as she came in the room and started laughing. "What's this, my welcoming committee?" she said. "Or just two nosey daughters, wanting to hear the gossip? It's way past your bedtimes – both of you!"

She didn't sound too cross, though. In fact, she looked happier than I'd seen her in ages. She even ended up letting us have a last cup of hot chocolate with marshmallows in before we went to bed. It seemed like Richard was going to turn out to be a GOOD THING!

Enough about my mum's love life anyway. Sorry! It's probably a bit boring for you but it was dead exciting for me. Let me get back to the main story and tell you about the pantomime instead.

Well, after all the gazillions of rehearsals we'd been having, it was starting to look really ace. Everyone knew their lines now – even Sarah King! – and the dancers and singers knew their songs and dances. The first test for us was on the last Monday afternoon of term – a dress rehearsal in front of the rest of the school!

The Sleepover Club

Of course, like all good dress rehearsals, there were a few disasters. When it came to the ball scene, Fliss somehow managed to tread on the hem of her ballgown and there was this great ripping noise as a big piece of material came away from her waistband. She went purple with embarrassment – especially as Ryan Scott was in the same scene as her – but like a true professional, kept dancing and smiling as if nothing had happened.

Then the other thing to go wrong was LYNDZ's fault! The Sleepover Club were certainly making their mark on this dress rehearsal... She and Matthew Silver, the two horses, crashed into each other by mistake and Lyndz went sprawling across the stage. Luckily, the audience seemed to think it was part of the show, and just cheered and laughed!

So that was the dress rehearsal over and done with pretty painlessly. Next, it was going to be the real McCoy, performing in front of all our mums and dads the following evening. Doing the pantomime in front of all the infants and juniors had been nerve-racking enough,

Merry Christmas, Sleepover Club!

but this was serious now. People had actually paid money to come and see the show... Gulp!

By the time Tuesday evening came around, it seemed like everyone backstage was feeling the same. People were putting their costumes on with shaky fingers, looking as pale as anything. It was a good job Mrs Somersby was on hand to put lots of make-up on everyone. At least she could make us look a bit less terrified.

Then I caught Lisa throwing up in the toilets, looking white as a sheet. Blimey, she must be REALLY nervous, I thought.

"Are you OK?" I asked, anxiously. She looked awful!

She wiped her mouth with some toilet paper. "I've got this terrible tummy ache," she said weakly.

"You'll be fine," I told her. "It's probably just nerves."

She shook her head. "I don't think so," she said. "You'd better get Miss Middleton – quick!" And with that, she was promptly sick all over again.

Miss Middleton came rushing into the

toilets at once when I told her. "Are you OK? Are you going to be able to do the show?" she asked, putting a hand to Lisa's forehead. "No, you won't – you're burning up!" she said. "I don't think you're fit to go on, Lisa!"

Lisa started to cry. "I really don't feel very well," she said miserably.

I felt so sorry for her, I almost cried myself. Our brilliant Cinderella, the star of our show... whatever were we going to do?

"Will we have to cancel the play?" I asked fearfully.

"No, don't worry," Miss Middleton said, frowning. Then she stared at me, with this thoughtful look on her face. "You know the script pretty well, don't you, Rosie?" she said.

"Well... yes," I said. "But—"

"How would you feel about playing Cinderella tonight, then?" she said briskly. "Lisa needs to go and lie down in the sick room. She certainly can't go on like this. And you've got a nice singing voice, so..."

"Wh-wh-what about Buttons?" I asked, feeling faint.

"I'll ask Alex McKay," she said. "As our other

prompt, he knows the lines as well as you. I'm sure he'll be fine."

"But..." I said, still not able to take all of this in.

"Come on, Lisa," Miss Middleton said, helping her to her feet. "Let's find you somewhere to lie down. Rosie – you'd better get yourself into make-up! You can do it, I know you can!"

Talk about knock me down with a feather! I was so stunned, I could barely walk back to the dressing rooms. "Lisa's ill – I've got to be Cinderella," I managed to mumble to the others.

"WHAT?" they all screeched. "No way!"

"Congratulations!" Lyndz yelled, half in her horse costume. She gave me a huge hug. "That's fantastic news!"

I grinned nervously. "Is it?" I asked. It was either fantastic news or the worst news I'd ever heard, I couldn't decide which.

"Brilliant!" Kenny said, punching me lightly on the arm. "You'll knock 'em dead, mate!"

"Break your neck!" Fliss said solemnly, looking beautiful in her (mended) dress.

"Break A LEG!" we all groaned at her.

"Ten minutes to go, everyone!" Mrs Weaver called from the next room. "Ten minutes! Please get your costumes on if you haven't already!"

We all looked at each other. Now I really WAS feeling nervous. The five of us had a big hug together. "We'll be great," Frankie told us. "We're all gonna be GREAT!"

It was the quickest ten minutes of my life – because before I knew it, Miss Middleton was calling for us to get in our places for the first scene. Then she made an announcement to the audience. "Ladies and gentlemen, we have a change in tonight's cast list," she said. "Tonight, Cinderella will be played by Rosie Cartwright, and Buttons will be played by Alex McKay."

AAAARRRGGHH! Now my heart was *really* thumping away! What would my mum be thinking about THAT?! I was just so glad that Frankie and Kenny were both in the first scene with me. We all squeezed hands before the curtain went up. This was it! I caught Alex's eye and he grinned at me. Fancy both of us humble prompts getting better parts at the last minute!

I know this will sound mad, but I honestly can't remember that much about the first few scenes. It all seems like a blur now. When I first started speaking Cinderella's lines, I kept trying to think about how Lisa had said them in all the rehearsals. My voice was a bit wobbly to begin with, but as the first scene finished, I remember thinking to myself, "This is going to be OK. We can do it!"

And do you know, as the show went on, I started to really enjoy myself. I'd been especially nervous about singing the songs, but when the moment came, I just went for it and got a huge cheer afterwards. And it was such fun doing scenes with Frankie and Kenny! I felt so relaxed with them, it really helped calm my nerves. In fact, as we got to the bit where I was trying on the glass slipper with Prince Charming, I was starting to wish the night would never end. I was enjoying myself far too much!

Mind you, the best bit was yet to come. The pantomime finished and then there was this huge ROAR of applause! Oh, it was *soooo* wicked, seeing everyone clapping like mad – it just sent a shiver down my spine. I'd never heard such a thunder of clapping! All for us!!!

We all bowed and went off stage, but the audience were still clapping and cheering, so Miss Middleton told us to go on stage and bow all over again. I caught my mum's eye and she gave me a huge wink. She looked as proud as anything, standing up, clapping fit to bust.

Wow! If this was what it was like to be an actress, give me more! I thought. It was a moment I was never going to forget!

As soon as the curtains came across, everyone started hugging each other and jumping up and down. Miss Middleton ran right over to me, picked me up and swung me round in the air! "You were great, Rosie!" she said. "Well done!"

"Thanks, Miss!" I said feeling dazed.

"Everyone was wonderful!" she said. "Alex – fantastic job as Buttons. Frankie – you were superb. Sarah – well done, word-perfect!"

I've got to say, it was one of the happiest moments in my entire life. Even Fliss was hugging me and telling me how good I was. And that's when I knew what my REAL Christmas wish was – to be an actress when I grow up! Now I'd had a taste of it, I wanted more – much more!

Well... that's about the end of the story, really. The next night Lisa was feeling better so she got to be Cinderella again, and I was back to being Buttons. I didn't mind too much, though. I'd had my moment of glory already, and knew that after all her hard work in rehearsals, Lisa really deserved a big round of applause, too. Christmas spirit and all that, eh?

I'll just have to wait for next year's pantomime now. You never know – I could be first choice for the starring role next time!

This is Rosie Maria Cartwright saying Merry Christmas and a very Happy New Year from all of us in the Sleepover Club. Have a great time – I know I will!

BUMPER EDITION!

24

Happy New Year, Sleepover Club!

It's party time! The Millennium is looming, and the girls plan a mega-special New Year sleepover. But what with Frankie's mum due to have her baby at any moment, and Fliss's mum with her Big Secret, nothing's going to end up going to plan. So what else is new...!!

Pop on your party hat and drop in on the fun!

Mystery gift attached!

Collins

www.fireandwater.com
Visit the book lover's website

Order Form

To order direct from the publishers, just make a list of the titles you want and fill in the form below:

Name ....

Address ....

....

....

Send to: Dept 6, HarperCollins Publishers Ltd, Westerhill Road, Bishopbriggs, Glasgow G64 2QT.

Please enclose a cheque or postal order to the value of the cover price, plus:

UK & BFPO: Add £1.00 for the first book, and 25p per copy for each additional book ordered.

Overseas and Eire: Add £2.95 service charge. Books will be sent by surface mail but quotes for airmail despatch will be given on request.

A 24-hour telephone ordering service is available to holders of Visa, MasterCard, Amex or Switch cards on 0141- 772 2281.

Collins
An *Imprint* of HarperCollins*Publishers*